THE CITY BANKERS' BROTHEL

The fascinating story of a £1m-a-year bankers' brothel

– Sorient Sigba –

An environmentally friendly book printed and bound in England by
www.printondemand-worldwide.com

This book is made entirely of chain-of-custody materials

www.fast-print.net/store.php

THE CITY BANKERS' BROTHEL
Copyright © Sorient Sigba 2014

A catalogue record for this book is available from the British Library

For comments or to order copies, please contact: sorient@hotmail.com

ISBN 978-178456-137-6

First published 2014 by
FASTPRINT PUBLISHING
Peterborough, England.

This book is dedicated to the glory of God and to Eucharia, Jason, Naomi, Marcel and Darren Sigba; without their love, support and understanding Sorient wouldn't have been able to get through his difficult times.

Contents

Introduction

T he story of how Mr. Freddie arrived at the idea of setting up the bankers' brothel was itself a tale of a complex personality.

Mr. Freddie's dream was to be a self-made man in the City of London. As he couldn't make it immediately in the mainstream economy, he decided to set up the bankers' brothel in the shadow economy. He knew that paying for sex is not illegal although selling it can be illegal and sex represented a new kind of entertainment in the City.

The brothel attracted rich punters, mostly bankers from the city. Many of the punters were people who occupied top positions with characteristics of shrewdness, miserliness and pompousness, pursuing lives of extravagance, excitement and enviably high living standards, with luxurious tastes in women.

The brothel was managed by Bella. Bella was a young woman who had limited her role to organising sex parties for the punters, managing the prostitutes, the drivers, the card boys and the money.

Mr. Freddie never thought the brothel would be raided one day. The relationships with punters and drivers were so normal and cordial, and Bella was so familiar with them, that the brothel could continue to operate indefinitely. He thought he was in a comfortable zone, but that thought was selfish and greedy. Everyone has enemies, but if you have a lifestyle like Mr. Freddie's, you're bound to attract envy.

In October 2011, the brothel was raided by the police, Mr. Freddie was arrested and the brothel was closed down.

Sorient Sigba

Chapter 1:
Mr. Freddie of the Bankers' Brothel

M r. Freddie was a middle-aged man trapped in an imperfect world. His only desire was to get the most out of life and make money in the city of London. He lived in a town outside London and had limited his life to looking after his children. He hated his life but loved his children. In his opinion, he was a perfectly good-natured man: talented, tactful, fastidious, patient, witty, unsuspecting, educated and intriguing. He was a gifted individual who tackled every task with a kind of ferocity.

Little was known about his obscure and pathetic character. He was born in Egbo-Uhurie in Ughelli, south of the Delta State of Nigeria. His age and date of birth were a mystery. He didn't possess a birth certificate. He could only tell the year he was born from a sworn declaration of age, depending on how old he felt at that moment. He had over ten sworn declarations of age.

To describe Egbo-Uhurie as a village might in truth be to exaggerate its importance, for it consisted of a few mud houses, one primary school, one secondary school, one major road, a shop, two churches and a town hall. He grew up on the family compound. Life moves on nicely and placidly in the family compound.

His grandfather was very popular with the villagers because of his magical powers. People would come to him for all sorts of treatments. He treated patients with religious incantations and traditional medicines for all sort of ailments. On the day of his grandfather's annual festival, tortoises would swarm onto the compound, white pigeons would flock onto the compound and his followers would come from various part of Nigeria. They would dance to folk songs and eat a cooked dish of fish from one pot and at the end of the day the pigeons and tortoises were released back into the bush.

Mr. Freddie, as an eight year-old boy, was particularly observant of his surroundings. The villagers liked him because of his easy-going ways; he was very respectful to the elders and they were fond of speaking of him as being a quiet and independent individual. He was very like his grandfather, but physically he was strangely like his mother, although his looks came from his father. He was little and slim like the mother, and had his mother's skin. He even had his grandmother's eyes and nose.

He was always sympathetic, gentle and generous. He would never hurt a fly. He had a beauty of expression, spoke fast with an accent, letting his voice die towards the end of his sentences.

Like any other child, he was a boy who had hopes and dreams, fears and worries. He loved playing football with his friends in the village. He did his assigned domestic duties: collecting drinking water from the pond, sweeping the floor and washing his dirty clothes. Sometimes he followed his grandmother to the cassava farm. He was very protective of his younger sister who also lived in the village with his grandparents.

To people of his village, he was known as a dedicated Christian. He regularly attended his local church built in the family's compound. His local church pastor was very fond of him. He lauded his dedication, good manners and spurious shyness.

Being pious was his obsession. Christianity pleased him because of its moral code and discipline. He believed so early in life that God existed, and realised that he couldn't live without God. On the other hand, the grandfather was the founder of a religious cult. He was engaged in a multitude of superstition and magical programmes. He was sophisticated, confident and prosperous, yet the family lived frugally.

Young Mr. Freddie ran naked and barefoot most of the time except when he went to school and Sunday Church service. It was an era when most children loved the feelings of nudity, and nature was greatly embraced in the village. He loved the village life, the routines and the atmosphere. He considered it to be the most exciting place in the world.

His grandfather was uncommunicative about his magical powers. Young Mr. Freddie believed there must be a wealth of undiscovered treasure behind that uncommunicative secret.

In the first few years after his grandfather's death, he was tormented by the old questions as to why he had allowed his grandfather's ancient knowledge to get lost. History tells us that the more advanced the civilization, the more easily it will die and leave little or nothing itself behind.

Mr. Freddie did manage to get a few tips from his grandmother. "You will do your family's name proud one day," the grandmother said. He didn't believe her because he was too absorbed in the present to think about the future.

The grandmother had a bit of soft spot for Mr. Freddie. She was always encouraging him to do well at school, which boosted his confidence and increased his determination. It was his grandmother who supported him through primary school. She kept him clean, dressed him exquisitely and gave him pocket money to spend. His teachers and classmates liked him. He would spend his pocket money on his classmates out of generosity.

To do well at school was something that was uppermost in his mind because he knew he was a clever boy. He did his school homework after his domestic duties.

Living in Egbo-Uhurie with his grandmother after the death of his grandfather was great for little Mr. Freddie. To be able to walk from his village surrounded by acres of rubber trees and find himself in the next village called Otokutu, where his mother lived, was heaven to him. There was no fear of being abducted or attacked by animals. It was safe for children to go out alone.

The only man in the village that belonged to his grandfather's magical society loved him. He would spend money on him regularly. He was the richest man in the village; he owned the village hotel and a transport company. He was a man of opulent appearance and charms. He was a philanthropist; he gave generously and lavishly to the local church and could always be counted upon for charitable donations.

Mr. Freddie left primary school in 1970. His grandmother wanted him to leave the village to further his education in the city. She decided to send him to live with his father. The father was living in Sapele and worked for African Timber and Plywood (AT&P). He was excited, eager to live city life and felt that the future would be bright. He was looking forward to his new journey in life. He believed that if a person was really cool with a big heart, that person would survive anywhere.

Soon after Mr. Freddie arrived in Sapele, his father enrolled him at a commercial school. Money was in short supply and the father couldn't afford the fees of the state secondary schools. Any feelings of apprehension that he had to study typing and shorthand instead of science disappeared. To his father, commercial school was the best alternative because secretarial jobs were readily available. He was prepared to study at his new school and experience city life.

During his second year at the school, his father was transferred out of Sapele to a remote village in the riverine area of the state. The village had no school, no electricity and no road. His father was allocated to a room in a suspended house above the river on a riverbank. The father left him behind in Sapele with his best friend to continue with his school. His father's best friend was a security guard who worked for the same company. Sometimes his father would send money to him and life was not as good as before until he finished studying at the school. The father was later transferred back to Sapele.

Life in Sapele as an unemployed young person was more or less laissez-faire and loftily nonchalant. Sapele at the period was established as a trading town in Nigeria. Its industries include the processing of timber, rubber, palm oil and have one of Nigeria's major ports. Nothing fantastic was happening as unemployment was still high due to population growth. His life of privilege was on unpredictable lines. He went to look for job in Warri. At about this time, he met a chief who gave him a job to work as his personal secretary. The chief was a rich man; he owned a hotel, a brothel and petrol stations. Mr. Freddie felt that he had something to offer the chief for his kindness.

The relationship with the chief was not one of employer and employee but that of father and son. Mr. Freddie felt he had come home. He managed the petrol stations and the brothel. He distinguished himself as a good son. The chief became his mentor and he was a disciplinarian. The chief could see something about Mr. Freddie's creative ideas, he advised him to further his education. He relished the advice and felt his dreams were about to be fulfilled. He decided to remedy the commercial school deficiency at a local adult education college. The pressure of work, socialising and a lack of effort made him to put that on hold halfway through the course.

Mr. Freddie really enjoyed working with the chief in Warri but, at the same time, his advice was something that always disturbed him and was a menace to his mind.

In 1981, he enrolled at Luba College in Ijebu-Ode, Nigeria to make up for what he was lacking for university admission requirements. At the final exams he got the grades and was happy with his performance. His intention had always been to pass the exams at one sitting, which he did. He came back to Sapele to meet his father after the final exams.

"I'm so proud of you, son!" his father said as he hugged him. Mr. Freddie felt so proud and marvellous. The fees he paid for the adult college had paid off. As the university year was months away, he was more than confident that he would gain admission.

Like with many dreams, there was disappointment; he failed to gain admission into the University of Benin. He took a job with the state secondary school in Sapele as a teacher of mathematics and commerce.

He taught at the school until he gained admission to study for a B.Sc. in Banking and Finance at the University of Calabar, Nigeria.

His life at university was extremely difficult and hard. His tuition fees and maintenance money was difficult to source, but as a person who was well-liked, he managed to work his way through and completed the degree programme.

After his graduation he went to Maiduguri and later to Lagos to complete the National Youth Service programme for the Nigerian government.

In 1987, the Organisation of African Unity sent him to the United Kingdom on a scholarship to study for a Ph.D. at Glasgow College of Technology, now Glasgow Caledonian University.

When he arrived in Glasgow, his first impression of Scotland was everything his childhood friend, Freeborn had told him. Freeborn worked at the British High Commission in Lagos and had visited Scotland in one of his annual holidays.

Mr Freddie studied Systems Analysis and Design at Glasgow College of Technology; and Software Engineering at the University of Stirling. He later enrolled at Jordanhill College, Strathclyde University and qualified as a teacher. He got married to his first wife in Scotland. He went to London after his marriage of two children broke down. He initially worked as a supply teacher in various schools until he got a full time teaching job. He had passion for teaching, but he was faced with the separation from his children. He was restless, sensing that he was missing the purpose of life but unsure what to do about it.

Being pious was no longer his priority. He gave up his teaching job to take custody of the children. He became a single parent on income support.

He had a dream and an idea. His dream was to become a self-made man. His idea was to be in self-employment with the prospect of steady work, a steady income, honour and respect, and become a philanthropist. Dreams, as all dreamers know quite well, do have disappointments. His dream to become a self-made man was in tatters

The sense of uncertainty grew stronger everyday as a single dad. Life at this time was becoming vigorously hard. He felt like a displaced foreign national. He became a cabbie in the shadow economy. He used the savings from working as a cabbie in the city to set up a software technology company.

Like many profit-making businesses, he started out with a reasonable business plan. He would provide an e-commerce website to anyone who needed a website. He purchased website templates, customised them and then sold them to anyone who needed one for a profit. That was one level of his operation. He also set up a payment system for chauffeurs, a platform where he accepted credit card payments on behalf of drivers for a fee. Soon after he set up the business, he sold various types of escort agency templates.

The plan to set up the bankers' brothel intrigued and at the same time excited him. It took time and effort to work out how to go about it. His vision of the bankers' brothel tends to fluctuate. Mr. Freddie's plan was to set up the brothel for punters who may use it for sex-related psychological problems or those who may use it to entertain clients in order to generate business. It was strange that the plan was embarrassing to him; the plan that the brothel would be for rich city bankers made it fascinating, not embarrassing.

Sometimes, the plan seemed to go smoothly and steadily. At other times it was plagued with difficulties, but he believed that he would succeed in setting up the brothel. He kept the plan of the bankers' brothel secret from his best friends until it was opened. Few people noticed what he was doing; he was shrouded from most people by a shawl of gossip which told them nothing about him. He was not happy to be known. Those who really knew him would be surprised to read about his story in the tabloid newspapers.

Given the assurance of perfect management by his friend Bella, Mr. Freddie assembled a team and set up the bankers' brothel. Each night Mr. Freddie would drive to the city to pick punters. Then he would return to the brothel with the punters to chat with the prostitutes and probably to have sex. Every now and again, he would drive to city strip clubs to market the brothel to the drivers. Bella would send text messages to drivers every night. The text message would read:

"Hello darling, are you okay?"

"Are you coming tonight?"

"I have twelve pretty women working tonight."

"See you later."

"Bye xxx."

Soon after it was opened, it attracted rich punters, mostly bankers from the city. The punters loved the brothel because it provided a discreet haven for them to enjoy the attentions of elegant, beautiful, intelligent women and there was a robust respect in the way the punters treated the prostitutes. The punters were trooping into the brothel between 1am and 5am. Drivers would drive them to the brothel from strip clubs with the promise of sex. In return, the brothel would pay the drivers commission.

Using prostitutes, using drugs, drinking and smoking became the established pattern of the City bankers' lifestyle. So, getting the punters to the brothel was easy. The atmosphere inside the brothel was always full of excitement, intoxicating and mirthful. The punters came to the brothel for various thrusts: some came to have sex, some came to take drugs and some came to have a massage or a bit of all three. The punters did things in the brothel that would be unthinkable.

Chapter 2:
Shadow Economy

Mr. Freddie began to work in the shadow economy. The shadow economy offered all kind of people the opportunity to make a living. Employment opportunities were wide-ranging and numerous for people, regardless of race, age, colour or sex. Imagine you're just being released on the street from prison with no support. What if you're immigrants with no right to work? What if you're unemployed for over two years? What if you're employed on a zero-hour contract with a family to maintain? What if you're destitute as a result of benefits cuts? It's hard to imagine, but these were the kinds of scenario some people faced in mainstream society and the shadow economy was readily available for making a living.

Mr. Freddie wasn't the name known to his family or his community in the United Kingdom. The name "Freddie" was an idea of a joke. Raja gave him that nickname when he entered the shadow economy workforce as a cabbie. Raja was a Pakistani immigrant, middle-aged and bright with a good sense of humour. Raja and his old BMW saloon car were popularly known amongst the cabbies who worked from strip clubs in central London. He knew everyone's secret stories.

Mr. Freddie and Raja became friends; they would loiter outside the strip club on Tottenham Court Road. They made jokes and laughed together frequently. Raja was the one who introduced him to the pussy market. The house where Raja lived with his family was bought from the money he made from the streets as a cabbie.

Raja coined the name "Freddie" for Mr. Freddie. It all began when Raja had a problem with the doormen for refusing to pay the weekly kickbacks for taking cab jobs from the strip club. Mr. Freddie usually paid his weekly kickbacks on time to hang outside the club for cab jobs. Raja refused to pay and branded the doormen "greedy". He was singled out and was banned from going to the club. Raja despised the doormen as a result of the ban but continued to go to the club for cab fares. Whenever the doormen saw him outside the club, they went nuts and scary.

One Thursday night, Raja was loitering, chatting and laughing among the drivers when he called the doormen greedy bastards; and this statement was overhead by one of the doormen who happened to be standing by the door of the club. The doorman called in three of his colleagues. The doormen came immediately and wrestled him down. The three of them together tried to hit him. They got him firmly on the ground and laid him facing the ground. He struggled, shouted and yelled for help, eventually he was let off. He was given a serious warning not to come back to the club. Raja then drove off unharmed.

The doormen had a good relationship with Mr. Freddie. He was a quiet person and paid his weekly rent. The way the drivers fought over fares made it difficult for him to get fares. He wasn't given the chance to get fares. He couldn't cope with the hustling and fighting involved in getting a fare.

One of the doormen named "Fred" was very sympathetic with him because of his commitment to pay his rent. He didn't like the way other drivers fought over customers, so he always stood up for Mr. Freddie. Sometime, he gave him cab jobs. Raja was envious and started to hail him "Mr. Freddie" after the doorman he hated most at the strip club.

Life as a cabbie was tough for Mr. Freddie. His major breakthrough came when he met a beggar and struck up an acquaintance with her. The beggar usually sat on a blanket beside the HSBC cashpoint machine near the strip club on Tottenham Court Road. He often went to have a laugh and stood with her for a couple of hours while waiting for cab jobs.

Her name was Amy. She was a young and pretty woman, freshly aware of her sexual attractions and more astonishing, quite happy to discuss them. She had beautiful blue eyes, prominent breasts and was blonde. She had a good sense of humour and Mr.

Freddie had never met a beggar quite like her. The idea of begging as a means of income seemed an effortless but potentially lucrative alternative to stealing. She reduced herself to a tramp and was substance-addicted.

Poor Amy always had stimulating conversation with her donors and was not embarrassed to ask passers-by for a bit of change.

"Can you spare me some change, please?" she said to passers-by with a smile. Passers-by would stop and throw some money into her plastic container. It was a breakthrough for her as the money continued to come.

As people came to recognise her, they felt more obliged to give her money out of pity. She was very pleasant and thankful to donors. Some of the punters thought they could get into her knickers. Whenever a conversation came to sex, she would call on Mr. Freddie and give him the punter to take to the pussy house. When he returned to the club, he would prepare an envelope with money to give to Amy, part of the money he had made from the punter.

Mr. Freddie continued to get cab jobs and continued to make money through these referrals. He could not believe his good fortune. His association with Amy became a success as he continued to get rich punters.

In many ways, his life as a cabbie became ideal. He met a variety of punters through her. Getting the rich punters was not onerous. Mr. Freddie remembered the night when Amy gave him a rich punter. She called him and said, "Hello, my beloved darling is looking for a pretty woman. Could you please drive him to a nice place?" Amy got up from the floor as Mr. Freddie was about to walk away with the punter, and said to the punter, "Look, don't take offence. It really doesn't matter whether it was me or another woman. I'm on my period. I'll see you later." Mr. Freddie winkled at Amy and drove the punter to Bella's Place. He made £1100 from the commission and the cab fare from the punter.

Mr. Freddie had adopted a strategy well suited for the shadow economy. He found Amy more desirable than anyone. Every night Mr. Freddie would stand at Amy's spot to chat and laugh with her. The doormen seldom bothered him for his weekly rent.

Amy usually arrived at the spot before him and promptly. She would be on her spot at 8pm and by 3am she had made £200. One night Mr. Freddie said to her, "You should count yourself lucky. I'd love to live like an ostrich, but I am in the wrong business. It's too boring driving the street of London like a headless chicken."

She laughed. Amy and Mr. Freddie were pleased with their acquaintances. For every one of Amy's punters, he would give her half of the money made.

Raja envied him for many reasons. Raja seemed irritated by the number of punters that he had taken to the pussy house. He met Raja at Bella's Place one night and suspected some personal innuendo. He sensibly resisted the temptation to confront him because an inner voice was urging euphoria instead of a fight.

Also, whenever he spoke to any of the doormen, it seemed to bite deep into Raja's soul and he resented it to the point of obsession. The doormen treated Mr. Freddie with more consideration than Raja. He had never deliberately tried to build up a relationship to smear him. He had never tried to collaborate with any of them to harm him. He was surprised by his behaviour.

Occasionally, Mr. Freddie would try to get the doormen to speak to Raja to resolve their differences, but nine times out of ten, Raja got a rude grunt. He said, "I was told not to come near the club and I was also told not to talk to them. That's the way it had always been." Mr. Freddie tried his best and there were times he was afraid of losing his mind. Something warned him against that happening. Survival on the street was always uppermost on his mind. "You've got to be focused if you want to survive in the shadow economy."

It was a very significant moment in his life as a cabbie. He was conditioned to expect the worst in life, to think of failure and humiliation. The thought of becoming a cabbie had never occurred to him. He only became a cabbie when he was living with his two children as a single dad. He was finding it hard to cope financially as he built up several debts. He remembered a Christmas Day where he had absolutely nothing to make it a special time for his children: no presents, no Christmas tree and no turkey. It was depressing, highlighting how difficult it is to live without money.

At this period he had just resigned from his teaching job, had custody of his children and was seriously looking for help of any kind. Mr. Freddie picked up his phone and rang John. John had been his cab driver at a mini-cab company in Peckham when he started to work as a supply teacher in London. They became close friends and he was the only person that could talk about his financial difficulties.

"Hello John, I'm sorry to bother you. I'm in trouble financially. Do you have any idea of how I can support myself and the kids?"

John replied, "To take up a 9am to 5pm job will be even harder with the kids."

John was very sympathetic.

"What else can you do with the kids?" asked John, "Can you drive at night?"

Mr. Freddie grinned. "Yes, I have a clean driving licence and nice car."

John went silent for the next minute, lost in his thoughts."

"How about becoming a mini-cab driver at night? Cash in hand! "I will show you the way. It is what I do for a living." John suggested. "And the money is good."

The more John spoke about being a cabbie, the keener Mr. Freddie bought into the idea of becoming a cabbie.

"Sound good and interesting to me," said Mr. Freddie, relieved that John had suggested it. It seemed a reasonable idea and a lucrative alternative than to try to find a job while he had custody of the children.

In the first instance, the thought of becoming a cabbie made him physically ill. He thought of the sheepishness and humiliation he would experience: the loitering, the jostling, the howling and the bustling. He imagined how he would feel if his mates or pupils were to see him as a cabbie. What would be his reaction? He could not say "I am cabbie." Shame would sweep over him, but he had no alternative. He gestured in agreement.

"Okay, I'll do that."

"Are you sure?" replied John. "When would you like to join me on the street?"

"Not tomorrow, I won't be there tomorrow. Next Friday will be okay. I will try it out", answered Mr. Freddie.

John was delighted at his response.

"You will have to meet me in central London on Friday at 12.30 in the night at Haymarket."

"When you get to Haymarket, park your car in any available space. Give me a call. I will give you directions for where to meet up."

"Thank you" Mr. Freddie said, "Goodbye."

On the Friday night, whilst the children were in their deep sleep, he slipped out of the house so as not to wake them. He had dressed smartly, wearing a dark suit, a white shirt and a dark tie.

Mr. Freddie drove his white Mercedes Benz car towards Trafalgar square in Central London. He drove aimlessly with the objective of looking for people who would take his cab. He was about to examine the quick possibilities of making money.

It's time you knew what happened next. Mr. Freddie's memory of that night would come back at odd moments. He was concerned about the humiliation, the gossip, the indiscipline, the envy and how mixed-up people got when it came to money. It was an experienced that would overwhelm anyone. It was the first time he would experience the shadow economy: the dark side of the new reality of our world.

Mr. Freddie spirits were high as he travelled into central London to look for cab fares. He stopped twelve times at traffic lights before he arrived at Haymarket. London has a network of traffic lights. As he got to Haymarket, he noticed a crowd of people mostly immigrants from Africa and Asia, hanging outside the door of a wine bar. He pulled to a stop and parked his car on a parking space opposite the wine bar. He rang John on his mobile phone to say that he had arrived. John told him to walk towards the crowd of immigrants and look for him.

Mr. Freddie wandered into the crowd. He found that the people were touts who were looking for fares from passers-by. They were like angry bees. Some were shouting, "Do you want a cab?" others, "Cheap cab for you." He was sad and felt very sorry. It was a new experience he had never witnessed. He had been completely isolated from society as he had been busy looking after his children.

He finally found John in the crowd and started to chat. One person seemed to recognise him. Anthony was his name. Mr. Freddie met him at his 40th birthday party. He was friendly and welcoming. He butted into their conversation and stayed with them for a long time. He asked Anthony, "Are you a cabbie too?"

He replied "Yes, when there is no real job."

John got a long distance fare from passers-by and left him with Anthony. Anthony was a perfectly natured man in his forties, an immigrant from Africa who had come to the United Kingdom to get a university degree and escape the civil war in his country of origin. The more Mr. Freddie spoke to Anthony, the keener he perceived the idea of becoming a cabbie in the shadow economy. Anthony asked Mr. Freddie to join them.

Mr. Freddie accepted eagerly. Anthony gave him a passenger going in his direction. The fare for the journey was £25 but he quoted £40. He dropped the passenger off and drove home to his children. He arrived home at 4am in the morning when the children were still asleep. He went to bed, but not to sleep. There was a burning desire in his head, the big decision to become a cabbie. Despite his self-denigration and qualifications, there was sense of heroism on his decision to become a cabbie in the shadow economy.

Next day at night, Mr. Freddie set off to central London while the children were asleep. He arrived at Haymarket and stood among his new colleagues. He loitered and laughed with them whilst looking left and right for passers-by for fares.

For a start, he had not reckoned the scale of embarrassment and humiliation he would experience. He stood at the entrance of the wine bar, approaching any passers-by. "Do you want a cab?" He could hardly believe he had been reduced to being a cabbie. He felt the lowest of the low.

Mr. Freddie's first customer that night was George. He drove him to Sevenoaks in Kent. The fare was £50, but the man paid £60. George liked Mr. Freddie and his car, so he made a deal to use him. Mr. Freddie was to pick him up at 2am from the wine bar and drop him at his house in Sevenoaks three times a week. He promised to pay £55 for each journey. All of sudden, being a cabbie had become his new profession.

At 3am when the streets were quiet, he drove his Mercedes Benz car around the City of London, keeping an eye on the people who signalled for cabs. He sometimes fought with passengers who refused to pay the overcharged fare in full.

Mr. Freddie met Raja on the street and they started to work together from one of the strip clubs on Tottenham Court Road. Raja would pick up a customer from outside the club and drive the customer to another strip club. The club would pay him commission.

Raja was making easy money from these runs. Sometime, he took the customers to a pussy house. There was a particular pussy house called Bella's Place. Bella, the owner of the house, ran the hookers. Bella had once been a hooker. Raja introduced Mr. Freddie to Bella and Bella's Place. Mr. Freddie was quick to make a coherent sense of Bella's Place.

His first experience of a pussy house had been when he picked up a man from the strip club, referred to him by Amy. The man introduced himself as Paul. Paul said he was an Englishman of Irish parents, educated at Eton College and Cambridge University. He was one of the City big boys. He worked as a stockbroker. He was sociable and well liked. At university, he had had a series of affairs. He also had a taste for drugs. He was a happily married man with two children.

Mr. Freddie drove him to Bella's Place. Inside the brothel, there were sofas that seated nine prostitutes. Paul sat on one of the sofas. Among the prostitutes was Laura. After Paul had sat down, he looked at Laura. She smiled at him and Paul smiled back at her. He said he liked the smell of her perfume, looking into her eyes. Laura stood up and held his hand to stand up. She gazed into his eyes with her alluring eyes.

"Let's go to the bedroom, Paul."

"Yes." Paul grinned and followed her to the bedroom.

Mr. Freddie stood in the kitchen with the other drivers, waiting for Laura to let him know whether Paul wanted to stay or not. Surprise, surprise, Paul paid cash for ten hours to stay with Laura. The market rate for sex at the time was £200 per hour.

Bella gave Mr. Freddie his commission for bringing him into the brothel.

He collected his commission and went into the bedroom to find out from Paul if he had to wait to take him home. At this time, Paul was already on top of her, fucking. As soon as he saw Mr. Freddie, he tried to control himself and pressed his cock against Laura without moving his waist.

"What is wrong, Mr. Freddie?" asked Paul.

"Shall I wait for you?" replied Mr. Freddie.

"I'm okay, you can go." Paul said, "See you, thank you."

Laura turned her head away from Mr. Freddie, trying to hide a wrap of cocaine. Mr. Freddie smiled and left the bedroom.

It was totally amazing to have earned £500 in such a short period of time. He had never earned anything of the kind. For once it seemed he and his children were happy and spending money on themselves. At this point, he felt nothing humiliating about being a cabbie, and no hatred for the shadow economy.

In July 2005, his second month on the street, Mr. Freddie stood with other cabbies outside the strip club in Tottenham when he spotted a man at the phone booth beside the club. He was looking at the hookers' photos posted on it. He bent his head so he could see clearly, then walked inside the phone booth.

Mr. Freddie approached him and said, "Hello Guv." The man was looking desperate for a hooker.

"Do you want me to take you to the hookers?"

The man smiled, "Are they beautiful?"

Mr. Freddie said, "Bella's Place has many beautiful women to choose from."

"Take me there," he said.

The man was someone Bella knew. George was his name. He was a nice man, so generous, so brave, so easily amused and so bad at fucking. He had a big problem with getting an erection.

"Come on." Mr. Freddie walked and George followed behind him to his car. He then drove George to Bella's Place. The brothel was glittering with beautiful women. George walked in and sat on the sofa while one prostitute came to him wearing a sequined bra, poking her breast into his eyes.

George smiled benignly and pointed to the prostitute called Sophie. Sophie held his left hand and led him to the bedroom. She smiled at him as both of them sat down facing each other, naked. Bella walked in to collect payment.

After an hour, Mr. Freddie realised that he had not been paid for his waiting time. He tried to call George's mobile phone but he must have switched it off. He went into the bedroom, to ask George if he needed anything but mainly, of course, to collect his payment for his waiting time. When Mr. Freddie glanced up, he was rather surprised to find George sobbing and looking frightened. The redness of his face, the awful gape of his mouth which seemed to be yawning, coupled with the groaning, grunting and moaning. He was tied to the bed, blindfolded with Sophie dressed in a black leather suit, vigorously giving him a blow job. She was pushing an oversized vibrator deep into his arsehole.

Mr. Freddie felt frustrated; he stayed calm and said to himself, "Moral evils come through misuse of freedom." He left the bedroom without asking for the money.

After the two hours George had paid for was up, he came out of the bedroom and walked out of Bella's Place straight to Mr. Freddie's car.

"Can you drive me to Southend-on-Sea?" George asked.

"Okay, Sir," Mr. Freddie replied. "I hope you had a great time?"

He entered the car.

"Thank you," George said, "I was greatly moved by the extreme kindness I experienced at the house." He was drunk and exhausted and fell asleep. He slept for most of the journey.

Mr. Freddie dropped him off, collected the fare for the journey and his waiting time. Surely, it had been another fascinating night. At home, Mr. Freddie rarely discussed his experiences in the city, not because he felt it was difficult to talk about, but because it never seemed necessary.

George became a friend of Mr. Freddie. Mr. Freddie found him an interesting and trustworthy person. He would call him whenever he was in town at night. Mr. Freddie very much valued his friendship.

Mr. Freddie began to enjoy the cabbie job as he began to make easy money. Life was never again hard. He could spend money on his children and had replaced his car. The months seemed to pass quickly but never, not for one moment, did he lose the determination to make money with his business skills and qualifications in the city. His dreams were still alive.

Three months later at 4am, Mr. Freddie was in his car driving home from Blackfriars Road. He spotted a man dressed in a grey suit, blue shirt and blue tie, sleeping on the pavement by Smithfield Market. The suit caught Mr. Freddie's eye and he pulled over and stopped. He tapped the man on his shoulder; he snored. He could barely move or speak. Mr. Freddie shook his body and said, "Are you all right?" He looked closely and was surprised to see it was George.

"What is the matter?" Mr. Freddie stood for few minutes, not knowing what to do. He shook his body again. "I am Mr. Freddie, do you want me to drive you to Southend?"

George briefly woke up. Mr. Freddie dragged him into his car and put him on the back seat. He was a big man of 120kg.

What happened next happened quickly and was a surprise to Mr. Freddie. George went into a deep sleep. He slept like a dead man: no movement, no noise and every effort to wake him up was fruitless. Mr. Freddie was confused, he decided to stay with him in the car until was a bit more sober. Eventually, he woke up after two hours. George was surprised to found himself inside a parked car with a black man.

George asked, "Who are you?"

Mr. Freddie replied, "I am Freddie."

George said,: "Why am I in this car?"

Mr. Freddie replied, "I found you sleeping on the pavement. I had to stop and dragged you into my car."

"I have been with you for over two hours?"

"Really."

George answered, "Drive to my office at Chancery Lane."

Mr. Freddie drove and dropped him at Fleet Street by Chancery Lane, beside the HSBC bank. As soon as he got out of the car, he said he had no wallet on him. He gave his mobile number and asked Mr. Freddie to call him at 2pm in the afternoon.

Mr. Freddie called him as requested. George asked him to come immediately to the same spot he dropped him off to collect the money for his fare and time. He jumped onto a train to meet him. When both of them met, George gave him £200 and said, "Thank you."

Chapter 3
Bankers' Brothel at The Mews

M r. Freddie's aspiration in life was to be self-made man. To fulfil his dream, he drew up a business plan for a competing idea to set up the City bankers' brothel at the Mews. The complete plan thoroughly explored every aspect of the brothel.

Mr. Freddie reviewed the importance of the brothel, identified the target market, described the facilities, calculated the expenses, described the operations, spelt out the requirements for management and projected the profit for the first year of operation.

Like many businesses, Mr. Freddie started out with a realistic market plan. He would provide an upmarket brothel to anyone who needed it in the City. That was one level of the business operation.

Under the plan, the punters would pay for the use of a prostitute for adventurous sex on an hourly rate.

The plan was elegant, profitable and simple. All it required was the punters to accept the quality of prostitutes. This would require detailed market research, something that evaded Mr. Freddie from the start.

Mr. Freddie visited various pubs, casinos and strip clubs to observe the night-life lifestyle of the punters. His observation revealed that debauchery was really going on in the City. He observed punters spending thousands of pounds on prostitutes. The majority of the punters were city bankers who earned £1-5m a year in bonuses and were spending £50,000 a month on client entertainment. Some of the punters lived on business expenses: payment for the use of prostitutes, drugs, food and champagne. They looked flashy, wore tailored suits and Rolexes and held piles of credit cards.

Mr. Freddie saw how desperately the city bankers needed prostitutes. The prostitutes he saw in the pubs were dolled-up young women in miniskirts, stilettoes and bleached hair. They were stunning, pretty and mostly from Eastern European countries.

This impressive and compelling business plan was an idea Mr. Freddie presented to his friend who had an interest in social business and projected the profit to him to be 20% of turnover. The friend afforded him considerable credibility and gave him financial and management support for the start-up. Another friend secured the lease of the property at the Mews for the brothel.

The property looked prepossessing enough; it occupied a beautiful three-bedroomed house in an industrial neighbourhood of Holborn in Central London. The house contained modern facilities: new glass kitchen cabinets, new faucets, flashing chrome stairs, glass showers and sinks and a marble floor.

The lounge was a large, open-plan room with the kitchen at the extreme end; it contained a cosy five-piece velvet suite in brown, a glass coffee table, 32-inch LCD television and security camera.

The kitchen area contained a chrome electric cooker, cupboard, white kitchen unit, sink, dining table with a red velvet cloth spread over it and four chairs. The kitchen had a door that led to the backyard garden.

The downstairs floor had a small cloakroom. It contained a washing machine and a tumble dryer. The cloakroom was sometime used as a bedroom. The upstairs floor had the three bedrooms. It contained one en-suite bedroom, two double bedrooms and one bathroom. Each of the bedrooms had a kingsize mahogany wooden bed with no headboard, a table lamp, standing fan, built-in wardrobes and chest drawers.

Bella, a resourceful person who had experience of managing a brothel, was hired as the madam of the brothel. Bella did virtually everything from recruiting pretty women to getting the prostitutes punters via cab drivers. Her real virtuosity was working on the phone. She was a born telemarketer, madam and organiser. She developed clever relationships with everyone. She operated the brothel as a community resource, providing specialised sexual services: blowjobs, dances, massage, sex and stripping. It was exactly what the City boys needed. She attracted beautiful women to the brothel, mostly from Eastern Europe and South America. These women were the ones willing to become sex donors for a premium. She was Mr. Freddie's long-time friend. Her success at managing Bella's Place had caught his attention and assured her respect.

Bella, a Brazilian, was 27 years old, about six foot tall, very pretty with long brunette hair, blue eyes and a large body. She managed the brothel in her own style and everyone was expected to co-operate. She was calm, hard, laid-back and friendly. She was popular with drivers and punters. She inspired loyalty among the prostitutes who worked in the brothel. She spoke with a trace of Portuguese accent. Bella recruited eleven women to work in the brothel for the opening: ten prostitutes and an assistant to help her with the daily routine. The prostitutes she recruited were willing to open their legs and spread them wide for the right amount of money, fun and prestige. The basic requirement to work in the brothel was the ability to speak good English, have a smooth body, elegant-looking beautiful legs, breasts of 34D, be an average height and have no tattoos.

The bankers' brothel made a difference to the prostitutes in the period of desperately financial difficulties.

Laura, one of the prostitutes was a young woman of 25 and a silicon-titted beauty. She was a Brazilian immigrant. She always dressed in a short black dress and wore neat make-up. Her dyed blonde hair was combed straight and tied with an elastic ribbon. She faked being solicitous. She spoke with a trace of a Portuguese accent. She had come to the UK to search for a better life and to support her family in Brazil. She was a former human resources manager in a computer company in Brazil.

Since she had arrived in London, getting a job had been a struggle. She had always been a woman who liked style. She was passionate about so many things – education, music, literature. She loved London. She could not recall exactly what had gone wrong. Her vision was to marry a British man to stay in the UK. When she started at the brothel, she always felt embarrassed whenever she was picked for a group sex party. She hadn't wanted her nakedness to be seen by other women until she became friendly with Clara.

Clara was another prostitute in the brothel. Clara was someone Laura knew reasonably well. Clara, a Brazilian, was a slim-built blonde with a bubbly character. She was in her early twenties. For almost a year after she arrived in the UK, she had been unemployed. Following this, she was involved in various relationships with men. In almost all of them, she had been subjected to domestic violence. She realised she could no longer continue to live the way she had been living. She took up a job as a stripper. Clara wasn't making enough money. She wasn't busy at the strip club. She went on to work for Bella at the brothel. Clara was very busy at the brothel. She was making good money and it was easy. She introduced her friend Amelia to Bella and she also became a prostitute in the brothel.

Amelia was an immigrant from Eastern Europe. A tall woman, she was long-legged, in her early twenties with short styled hair and always wore a black mini-skirt. She was well educated with a pleasant sense of humour. She was very formal in her manner and speech. She spoke with trace of a Russian accent. Amelia fancied Mr. Freddie and became a friend of Mr. Freddie. He would pick her up from the brothel and drop her at home whenever she asked for a lift home. Mr. Freddie would also buy food for her in the night. He could have had quite a few one-night stands with Amelia. It was easy and free.

Giselle, another prostitute, was known for her big boobs. Giselle was born in Venezuela with the name Isabella, but she changed her name when she became a prostitute at the brothel. She had come to the UK to work so that she could support her daughter the best she could. She had permed brown hair, about shoulder length and wore a very tight dress. The dark nipples of her tits were always exposed. She was bright, crazy and funny. She had a slim body and thin legs. The nipples on her big silicon boobs and dress were fixtures at the brothel. Giselle knew that every client fancied her. She spoke without any trace of an accent.

In all the time Mr. Freddie was in the brothel, he never really got to know any of the girls beyond the superficial, except Amelia and Erika.

Erika was most known for her leadership and awe-inspiring sex acts. She was a Brazilian immigrant. She was a medium-built blonde woman with a bubbly character. She was in her mid-twenties and perfectly natured. For almost all of the six months since she had arrived in the UK, she had been unemployed. She realised she could no longer continue to live unemployed with no money.

Firstly, she took up a job as a stripper at one of the gentlemen's clubs in the city to tackle her debts. She wasn't busy at the stripper's club.

Secondly, through word-of-mouth, Bella offered her a job. Erika became a popular prostitute. She spoke good English with a trace of a Portuguese accent. She attracted a lot of punters and was making easy money.

She was like a mother figure in the brothel. She was always worried if a prostitute wasn't making money. She would show the prostitutes how to smile to attract customers. She also introduced Katharina and Maya to work in the brothel.

Katharina was a young and shy Hungarian. She sat on her own most of the time in the brothel. When customers arrived, she would look at them with a drowning expression, and then softly say, "Hello". At times she would smile to seduce customers to pick her. She wore an expression of such earnestness that it seemed impossible to refuse her when she smiled. She was a real chic.

Maya was a twenty-four year-old, medium-built and pretty woman. Her arms were as thick as a man's, and when she fucked the whole bedroom would shake. Most punters liked her sexual acts because she fucked like a rabbit. Like Erika, she was always worried if a prostitute wasn't making money. She would give out tips on how to do their make-up, how to give a sensitive blow job, how to take or pretend to sniff cocaine with a punter and which punters to turn down. If you looked at her and the other prostitutes, there was pleasure and benevolence on her face.

In October 2005, the city bankers' brothel was opened for business. The opening began with a celebrating buffet. There was plenty of food, snacks and pretty women. The importance of the relationship between drivers, the madam and Mr. Freddie was vital to the success of the brothel. The punters who would come for sexual services were carefully selected to minimise the chances of a problem developing in the brothel.

The operation of the brothel was easy and simple. Typically, customers came to the brothel with a driver, the orders were taken by the madam and the prostitute offered the sexual services for a fee. The brothel was full of pretty women willing and eager to open their legs for the right amount of money, fun and prestige. The presence of pretty women gave the brothel the atmosphere of a flower garden. The brothel quickly became a popular house for rich punters. More and more punters queued up for the

11.30pm opening. The bankers' brothel served a thousand clients in just a year.

The brothel business attracted its own spin-off businesses for drivers, card boys and drug dealers. Drivers would hang around the brothel to look for taxi fares at exorbitant prices. Card boys would hang around the brothel to provide credit card payment. Some people would come to sell drugs to the punters and others to sell sex toys and clothes to the prostitutes.

Bella the madam ran the house, did the accounts, attended to drivers, organised the prostitutes and entertained the punters in her own way. The punters lauded her respectful manners of speaking, her spurious shyness and her little curtsies. Bella was a modern businesswoman who had earned admiration for careful management and an eye to make a profit for the brothel.

The brothel began to make a profit after two days of opening to the city bankers. Every night there were so many punters desperate to fuck. Bella was always rushing up and down the stairs. There was so much noise; she had to keep the noise level down. It was just the way of doing things in the brothel.

Mr. Freddie remembered two punters who visited the brothel on two separate occasions, who made him feel more despondent than anything else. He discovered later a number of oversea bankers do visit the brothel.

One he knew only slightly; he used to see him occasionally in the brothel. He was well known to Bella. He was brought in by a driver.

Erika asked the visitor "What is your name?"

The visitor replied "Gordon."

"Where are you from?" asked Erika.

Gordon replied, "I'm from Canada."

Mr. Freddie was listening to every word. Gordon asked, "What do you have to offer?"

"Well, for £300 I will give you a good time for one hour." She said it carelessly, smiled at him and her eyes sparkled humorously.

"Okay," Gordon replied. Erika led him upstairs to a bedroom. He spoke to Erika for about thirty minutes, then fumbled in his pockets for his wallet. He checked his Rolex watch and gave her £300 for one hour and £100 as a tip. He demanded a kiss and to fuck her arsehole.

Erika said, "No, not allowed in this house." Nobody knew what happened next, but Gordon left the bedroom and the house without saying a word.

The second man made Mr. Freddie feel embarrassed. He was driven to the brothel from a nearby strip club by one of the drivers. The punter was a guy Mr. Freddie once met in the brothel. He was known to the house as Howard. He was an American from New York. He came to London quite a lot to transact business in the city. He came to the brothel a few times, and each time he was greeted enthusiastically by Bella. At the time of his arrival, there were eight prostitutes in the house. It was 4am in the early hours of the morning. Among the prostitutes were Sophie, Katharina and Gisselle. Katharina was dancing, wearing nothing but a G-string. Sophie and Gisselle sat on the sofa watching a movie on the television. After Howard had sat down, Katharina smiled at him. He smiled back. Howard picked Katharina straight away. She led him to the bedroom upstairs.

What happened next was a surprised to Mr. Freddie. Often Katharina would shout at Howard. "You can do better, you whelp!"

"You're lazy!"

"Turn your back!" The talk followed a ferocious flogging. Howard had paid Katharina to be flogged. There was something pathetic about Howard. Mr. Freddie was compelled to remain in the house after the closing time of 5am. Howard also remained after Katharina had finished with him, waiting for the train station to open. Howard sat on the sofa facing the television, reading a book with a sort of steady fierceness.

"Are you alright?" Mr. Freddie asked.

Howard replied, "Sex and Fetishism, it's a refreshing book."

Mr. Freddie starred at him and the book. Howard was a man full of knowledge and misinformation. Mr. Freddie was disgusted by what he came to do in the brothel.

Mr. Freddie got so lucky with the brothel. For the drivers who brought punters to the brothel, it was like celebrating Christmas every day. Every day they were making good money from the brothel. Mr. Freddie and the drivers became trusted friends and every day was cool. Mr. Freddie was trustworthy, generous and marvellous.

The drivers were like wolves and they sometimes fought each other. It was funny the way the drivers went about their business. They didn't feel a sense of humiliation or embarrassment. Their only thoughts were focused on the money to be made. Perhaps that was a good thing for desperate people. One of drivers, Tosan was on top of the game. He was a good hunter. He would drop a punter, and a few minutes later he was back to the strip clubs to hunt for other punters.

Tosan was Mr. Freddie's favourite driver. Tosan was born in London. His parents were Nigerian immigrants. He was brought up in a humble manner and completed both his primary and secondary school. He spoke with a trace of a South London accent. Soon after he finished secondary school, he was caught up in a gang and went to prison for drug dealing. He was released onto the same streets where he had offended in the first place with virtually no money and very little support. In an attempt to rebuild his life, he had become a cabbie, the only occupation he knew.

Bella the madam liked him immensely. She liked him because he had easy-going ways and attentiveness. He usually helped Bella empty the bins, clear the used condoms in the brothel, tidy the bedrooms, put away credit card machines and make indignant punters co-operate. He was very handy to Bella. Tosan had special punters that spent big in the brothel and he earned good commission. He was living a far more comfortable life than he had experienced. The prostitutes were fond of speaking to Tosan as "being a hard man and friendly". They would call on him at any time there was trouble in the brothel. Tosan was always ready to help. The prostitutes believed Tosan had a shrewd and dangerously candid tongue and a certain brutality of expression that was justly feared, unlike most cabbies who brought punters to the brothel.

One day, Tosan invited Mr. Freddie to his house. Mr. Freddie went to visit him one Saturday afternoon. He lived in a cleaned one-bedroom flat in Abbey Wood. He was glad to see Mr. Freddie in his house. Mr. Freddie throat's felt yummy when he smelt the spicy odour of good African cooking. After a while, Tosan offered him roasted tilapia fish, fried plantain and a bottle of red wine. Mr. Freddie and Tosan ate and drank together with a very good appetite. They were talking and laughing. Mr. Freddie asked him about his relationship with Bella. Immediately the pleasure of being welcomed to his house went out of his face. Mr. Freddie discovered from the daily work sheets that Bella and Tosan were using tricks to charge the punters. Regular and repeat punters' commission was paid to Tosan as the driver who brought them. We are talking about huge sum of money. The trouble with Mr. Freddie was that he thought other people couldn't tell what he was thinking.

"You have taken my position here, and I thought you were working with me. Please don't run the house as your own," Mr. Freddie said warningly.

Tosan gave him a sideways look. "You can't just build opinions like that. You won't do any good not trusting your madam. You won't do any good if you sack Bella. She is the pillar of the business and honest." He continued a shrewd side glance, but Mr. Freddie kept his face stolid, a commonsense move to avoid confrontation.

Mr. Freddie left his house with profound disgust. Tosan became spiteful and contemptuous of his fellow cab drivers.

Chapter 4
Cab Drivers

The cab drivers who worked in the shadow economy provided another kind of service: transporting punters from pubs, strip clubs, hotels, connecting them with prostitutes and facilitating the provision of sex, drug and champagne.

The brothel relied on the drivers for business. The drivers had the sale techniques. The unique selling point for the bankers' brothel was that it was an "after party" club. So, Mr. Freddie drew up a list of twenty drivers and gave it to Bella.

Bella would send out text messages to the selected drivers such as, "10 beautiful flowers". That meant the brothel had ten beautiful women for the night.

The message was coded for general misunderstanding. She would speak to the drivers on the drawn lists. She would tell them the number of prostitutes that were working that night. She would give them the address at the Mews and the mobile telephone number. She made it mandatory for the drivers to call before bringing customers to the brothel.

The cabbie industry in the shadow economy was worth over £1 billion a year. It employed over 100,000 cab drivers. It was difficult to put an exact market value as many of the cab drivers were self-employed and did not provide publicly available returns on their income. The cab drivers who worked for the bankers' brothel were a mixture of immigrants from Africa and East Asia, people who had been judged as incompetent in supervised employment in the mainstream economy. To be a "driver for the bankers' brothel" was the only occupation they knew. The cab drivers owned their cars and only worked at night for the bankers' brothel. The drivers had duly accepted a belief of inferiority and immorality to make a living.

In desperation for fares and commission, the drivers would hang around outside strip clubs at night waiting to prostrate before the city bankers for pussy business. Outside the entrance of the city clubs, the drivers demonstrated how mixed-up people could behave when it came to money matters. The drivers were like wolves that howl. Indians think the howls of wolves are the lost souls of the dead trying to return. The drivers howl before they hunt for the city bankers. They howl out of the huge commission to be made from the bankers' sexual lifestyle. The drivers acted as brokers for both the brothel and the punters.

Mr. Freddie worked in the cabbie industry and met some amazing and inspiring people in the shadow economy.

One of them was Bashir. Bashir was known for his determination to survive. He was born in Afghanistan. He was an educated immigrant. Once he'd been an army commander. He wanted to work as a prison warder but could not get a job. He had always been a man who liked style. He was passionate about so many things and he loved London. His vision was to own a restaurant in

Central London. So what had gone wrong? He could not recall exactly.

How he had decided to become a cab driver wasn't a surprise. Bashir had met an old friend, Hamza. Hamza arrived in the United Kingdom at the same time as Bashir from Afghanistan. Hamza had been working as a cab driver since his arrival. He only worked nights for the city bankers' brothel. The two-bedroom flat where he lived with his family in West London was purchased with the money he made from working as a cabbie for the bankers' brothel.

Bashir's reaction to Hamza's situation made him say, "It is time to say boo to the goose". Instead, the respected former army commander became a cab driver. At night, he would drive to central London, hang around pubs and tout for passers-by for fares. He charged twice the fare of a journey, even if he didn't know where he was going. He relied on the passenger for directions. He became known among cab drivers and punters in the city. He would do anything for his punters. As a result, he had a lot of regular punters.

He was introduced to the bankers' brothel at the mews. Sometimes, he would take his punters to the brothel. He became knowledgeable on how to negotiate his way through the shadow economy. He was happy and found London an attractive place to live.

After working for two years as a cabbie, he bought the house of his dreams in Afghanistan and set up a kebab shop in central London, employing six people and paying his taxes.

One of his colleagues in the shadow economy was Onye. Onye was an immigrant from Nigeria. He was born in a town called Aba. His parents were comfortable. His father owned and ran a transport business. He grew up in a solid, three-storey house in Aba. The house had a field in front, a backyard with palm trees and a high fence all around. He had gone to one of the top universities in Nigeria, where he studied Business Administration. He graduated with a second class degree and worked with the father.

He came to the United Kingdom to study for ACCA. He completed the course, but failed the final exams several times through a lack of interest. He decided to work. He was rejected from various companies on various grounds. He could not secure the job of his dreams. He drifted around selling drugs for a year. He took a variety of jobs. He worked as a security man, a barman and in a warehouse for £100 a week.

He met Bashir on the street of London by accident. Bashir was a successful cabbie because of the number of punters he took to these brothels. He was an inveterate liar who lied to punters only to transport them to the brothels. He was always well dressed, usually in a three-piece grey suit, a tie and expensive black shoes. Bashir told Onye how many punters he took to the brothel and the amount of money he made in a night. Onye saw the lifestyle of Bashir and decided to become a cabbie. He was introduced to the lucrative bordello business in the city.

One of his breakthroughs was when he met a punter called Gary outside a strip club in Soho. He was laughing and loitering with some drivers outside the gate of the club when he saw Gary from afar. He was pissed and stood at the corner of the road leading to the back of the club. He was waiting for one of the dancers who he had given £1,000 for the promise of sex. Onye approached him and Gary walked away from him quickly and silently. Of course, so many people would feel uneasy when approached by a stranger. Gary assumed Onye was about to pull a scam; besides, he was clouded by confusion.

Onye came back to hang out with the drivers. One of the drivers whispered to Onye "That man he recently spoke to was a big fish." Onye had mixed feelings, wondering how he could get to Gary and make money from him.

At 2.30am, punters started to leave the strip club as it got to the closing time. When the club was totally empty and no one else was around, Gary lost hope of the stripper he had given money to. He was depressed that he had been scammed. He decided to drown his sorrows and look for someone to share his disappointment with. Gary went to look for Onye at the entrance of the strip club. He walked hastily towards the entrance where the drivers were still standing. Onye saw him and ran after him. He had guessed that there was problem long before Gary angrily dismissed him. The bitter disappointment Gary felt at losing his money was shown by the glare on his face. £1,000 was not a great deal by Gary's standards, but that is pussy. Onye suggested Freddy's after party club where he could get pretty women for a fuck; he happily nodded his head in agreement. He took Gary to his car, entered the car with no hesitation and drove him to Freddy's. Inside the car, Onye smiled to show him that he really meant business. He drove through Shaftesbury Avenue to Holborn via Gray's Inn Road to the brothel. As soon as they got there, both walked inside. Gary sat on the sofa opposite the TV beside a prostitute called Amelia. Onye went to sit with other drivers in the kitchen area.

Bella the madam offered Gary a bottle of beer. Bella introduced the prostitutes to him, explained the rules of the brothel, and asked him to pick. It took a moment for him to calm down.

"I'm not interested," said Gary. "This is not a bar." Bella repeated with relish that it was an a after party club.

Gary whispered to Amelia, "Is it true that I can have sex with any of you?" Amelia pinched him.

What happened next was a surprise. He quickly struck a deal with Amelia. She pulled Gary up off the sofa and led him to the bedroom upstairs. Both of them sat on the edge of the large bed facing each other.

She asked, "How many hours would you like to spend with me?"

Gary replied, "How much cash do you need for the whole night?"

She said, "Ten hours at £300 per hour, is that okay?"

Gary nodded in agreement. Amelia called on Bella to collect the money.

Sorient Sigba

Gary gave Amelia some extra money as tip. She handed him a pink bathrobe and hangers to hang his clothes. Both of them got naked with the lights on. Amelia's nipples was pointing up and down, Gary gave her a mirthful laugh and unable to think what to say, he started to touch her boobs, feeling her boobs with one hand and grabbing her arse with the other hand. Amelia watched him. He twisted his hand around her pussy with his eyes on her eyes.

"Please let's fuck." Amelia suggested. She pounced and grabbed him putting the head of his cock into her mouth. She drew as much of his cock without gagging her mouth on it. She slowly lifted her head as she stared at him intently for a few minutes and made a sound as she released the cock from her mouth. She smiled close to Gary's face.

Gary then said, "I need more of that!"

She continued to suck and lick all over his cock, balls and even dabbed her tongue in his arsehole. For the next five minutes or so, he couldn't take anymore.

He grumbled, groaned and screamed out the name of his wife "Anna ooooooo!"

"Fuck me!" she whispered.

Gary started to finger her. He stuck his tongue inside her pussy and licked the edge of it. He dropped his hands and gripped the roundness of her buttocks. She stood up slowly and Gary rose with her. She pulled his arms around her back. She turned around, bent down and leant her buttocks against his penis. She signalled that she was ready to receive his cock, doggie style. Gary then plunged his cock into her pussy, fucking her from behind to give it a lot of depth. He continued to hit the clit spot while she was winding her waist. Amelia's thighs started to shiver, signifying that she was about to have an orgasm. She moaned, groaned and exploded with a massive orgasm. Gary came after her. There was a short silence. Amelia suppressed a small smile and Gary immediately pulled out his cock after he poured his sperm.

"You're terrible." Amelia smiled, not expecting an answer from Gary.

"Thank you, I love it. All I ever needed tonight," he declared, "was a beautiful woman like you. I was scammed by a stripper before coming to you." Amelia was delighted with the statement. "But what did the stripper do to you?"

Gary replied: "Well, she ran away with my thousand pounds."

Amelia asked: "How beautiful was she?"

Gary said: "She wasn't as beautiful as you."

Amelia replied: "What?" She looked at him blankly for a few seconds before smiling. "That's good for you men. So, this is why you have come to me?"

She got dressed, pulled her hair up and quickly applied some make-up

Gary got dressed too. Amelia said to him, "Let's go to the lounge." She then led him down the stairs. Gary followed her down the stairs into the lounge where Mr. Freddie was chatting with the drivers at the kitchen area.

Gary stared at Mr. Freddie for few moments. "I'm done," he said, "Time for me to go home. Can you arrange for someone to take me home?" Mr. Freddie said he should sit down while he called the driver who had brought him. Onye wasn't answering his phone. Mr. Freddie suggested he would arrange for a taxi to drop him. He wasn't ready to wait any longer, but asked for directions to where he could get a black taxi. Mr. Freddie gave him directions to Gray's Inn Road. He walked out towards the front door and said, "Goodbye" to everyone. Mr. Freddie opened the front door, he walked out and slammed the door.

Onye became a successful cabbie. He did not feel right unless he met his target of £500 a night. He worked in the shadow economy for three years as a cabbie. He built a solid three-storey building in Nigeria. He gave up being a cabbie to become a card boy - providing a credit card payment facility for buying sex in brothels.

Chapter 5:
Card Boys

T he city bankers' brothel accepted a lot of payments by credit card every night. Credit cards had become a popular method to make purchases in the brothel. The excessive lifestyle highlighted by wealthy activity in the city, had encouraged city bankers to use credit cards for a wider range of expenses: sex, drugs, alcohol, gambling etc. The credit card industry had a strong growth in the shadow economy.

The credit card industry consisted of card issuers who provided the credit cards to the customers who came to the brothel, and merchant acquirers who issued credit card equipment to the card boys to enable them to accept credit card payments.

Financial deregulation reduced the barriers to entry into the credit card industry, so it was easy for card boys to get credit card equipment from the banks. The card boys would apply for the credit card reader machines with fictitious businesses such as hairdressing, courier services, entertainment clubs etc.

The card boys provided the credit card reader machines to the bankers' brothel at a rate of 30% commission. When the card boys received £780 for two hours of sex, they would pay £600 cash to the brothel on the spot. They would receive £180 as commission. Although the card boys provided the payment services for the brothel for a profit, they sometimes lost money when a customer cancelled a transaction or when their bank withheld their money for it being a fraudulent transaction. There were many people who worked in the shadow economy as card boys. The card boys mainly provided services to the brothels in the city.

Palik was one of them, a close associate of Onye. Palik was an unemployed cab driver who hung around the city bankers' brothel. Sometimes, he picked up a few pounds selling Viagra with a routine of ripping off punters by selling a tablet for £20.

Palik, a Briton from Bangladesh was known as a muscle man. He was powerfully built, weighing 40 stone and had a tanned complexion. He used to be a doorman.

Mr. Freddie found out he had been to prison for six months. He had just been released on the street without support. He couldn't get a supervised job because of his criminal record. Palik approached Mr. Freddie to ask if he could bring a credit card wireless terminal to use in the brothel. He looked serious and desperate.

Mr. Freddie replied, "Good idea, but only if you have the cash to pay straight away. Do you have the cash? How much cash can you bring every night?"

"£5,000," Palik said. He showed him a worn-out A5 envelope full of £50 notes.

Mr. Freddie gave the go-ahead. After all, punters came to the brothel with piles of credit cards of different colours, but limited cash.

Bella the madam of the brothel embraced the idea. Palik became a card boy for the bankers' brothel. He provided the wireless payment terminal for commission on every transaction value. He got the terminal from his uncle, who owned a groceries shop in Southall.

Palik began to process payment for the brothel. When a punter was charged £300 for an hour of sex, he would add his 30% commission and processed £400 on his terminal. He reimbursed the brothel with the £300 and keep £100 for his commission. He had to pay the merchant acquirer a merchant service fee for arranging the transaction. After three working days, Palik was reimbursed by the merchant acquirer.

In a week, Palik processed on average £20,000 worth of transactions. In a month he earned commission of over £15,000. He built a modern hotel complex in Bangladesh. The hotel he built was from the money he earned in a year working in the shadow economy.

Chapter 6:
City Bankers and Sex

T he penis and vagina are the most sensitive parts of the human body, a valuable natural resource and as vulnerable as the humans who carry them.

Sex represented a new kind of entertainment and City bankers entertained clients in the bankers' brothels in order to generate business. For its grime and sleazy atmosphere, the bankers' brothel at the mews became a focal joint in the city. The city bankers trooped in every night and queued up waiting for adventurous sex. They were prepared to spend big on the prostitutes. They were the people who taught the prostitutes conformity without imagination. After all, sex is good for the health, as a treatment for obesity and exercise for mental awareness. Sex became a form of healthy exercise that can help prevents stress and diabetics. Many bankers could not get it from their partners due to the nature of their job.

Mr. Freddie understood that the principles of moral banking had been violated by the city bankers. Night after night city bankers were seen in strip clubs and in brothels sleeping with prostitutes. The city bankers' addiction to sex, drinking, and drugs made businesses in the shadow economy which embraced immorality. To expose the hypocritical iniquities of the city bankers was not the main thrust. The city bankers involved the good people in the city in the sorrowful guilt of upholding immorality.

City bankers came to the brothel to have sex, some came to receive blow jobs, some came to buy prostitutes' pee, some came to have massages, some came to be dragged like a dog, some came to be beaten up like a horse, some came for masochism, some came for voyeurism, some came to entertain clients, some came to drink champagne and some came to buy the prostitutes' underwear: sexual acts, practices and behaviour that lay outside normal or traditional sex.

Use of prostitutes became the common norm among the city bankers. Sex reflected something missing in the city bankers' relationships.

The concept that paying for sex exploits women did not prevent the city bankers from using the brothel. Unfortunately, they were trapped in a lifestyle of shameless practice. They made themselves available for cabbies to be picked from various strip clubs late at night and to be driven to the bankers' brothel for sex.

Mr. Freddie was always around the brothel to offer assistance to the punters and Bella the madam. He made sure that the brothel was calm and peaceful. He enjoyed the lifestyle and mingled with prostitutes and rich punters. The excitement and glamour of the brothel began to affect him. He could have had quite a few one night stands. It was free and easy for him. The whole atmosphere - the sight of seductive pretty women, the freak behaviour of the drivers and the punters - was intoxicating. He had never experienced that lifestyle. It made him realise that up to that point, he had had no knowledge of the thriving shadow economy and what happened within it. The sense of unreality grew stronger every day. He felt he had entered a different world.

Sex, drugs and champagne became the established pattern of the city bankers' life. Such a lifestyle had been developed and embedded in the city financial market. The city was being motivated by financial bonuses and penalties. Bankers were seen awarding themselves huge bonuses and debauchery was going on every night in the city.

There were happenings inside the brothel that Mr. Freddie considered surprising, freakish and unthinkable. It was on a Thursday morning at 1am when Mr. Freddie was driving to the brothel from his home in the south east of London. He drove passed the brightly lit local strip clubs at Holborn. The sight of several of the drivers outside one of the strip clubs persuaded him to stop to say, "hello." Outside the club, it was like mob rule. The drivers were waiting to take rich punters to the bankers' brothel. He met the drivers and was greeted warmly. The drivers were surprised to see him. He rarely went there at night to hang out with the drivers since most of the time he was at the brothel helping out. He started to chat with one of the drivers, Bashir.

Mr. Freddie was chatting with Bashir, when a black cab pulled over. Mr. Freddie quickly recognised him. He was Shaun, a city banker. Mr. Freddie knew him better than every driver hanging outside the entrance of the club. He had been to the bankers' brothel on more than two occasions. He was in his late forties. Mr. Freddie nodded to him in his usual casual manner.

"Do you know me?" Mr. Freddie asked him

"You're Mr. Freddie."

Mr. Freddie smiled and nodded. "Yes, I didn't expect to see you in town tonight."

They all laughed and joked. Shaun turned towards the club, after he had closed the door of the black cab. He said to Mr. Freddie, "Thank you for the other night. My mate and I had great fun."

At this time, the club was totally empty exception of the drivers hanging outside the club.

"The club has closed," said the doorman to Shaun. He walked back to Mr. Freddie and asked him to take him to the bankers' brothel.

Shaun whispered, "Today is my birthday. I need a couple of blondes, able to fuck like rabbits." The expression on his face was full of excitement.

Shaun and Mr. Freddie exchanged glances. Mr. Freddie asked Shaun to follow Bashir into his car for a drive to the brothel. Shaun followed Bashir, entered his blue Mercedes Benz car and was driven to the mews.

Mr. Freddie sent a text message to Bella, the madam at the brothel.

"Bashir is bringing a regular customer. A big fish, do you have a free room available? He was there two weeks ago and stayed with Giselle. Please call in the card boys; he had couple of credit cards on him."

Bella replied: "The small room is free and Giselle is not busy."

Mr. Freddie was just approaching the corner of the road leading to the brothel when his mobile signalled an incoming text message.

It was from Bashir: "Mr. Freddie, where are you?"

Mr. Freddie replied, "I will be with you in ten minutes. I drove to Edgware road to buy a kebab for the girls."

Bashir wrote: "The customer and I are waiting for you outside the mews in my car."

Mr. Freddie arrived at the mews and rang the doorbell. Bella opened the door for Mr. Freddie. Mr. Freddie beckoned the driver and Shaun inside the brothel. Shaun was greeted vivaciously by the prostitutes. Two punters were in the brothel having a big party. The atmosphere inside was intoxicating. Shaun sat on the sofa opposite a low glass table beside Giselle and Amelia. He stared at Amelia and prompted her to tell him about herself.

"Hello honey!" she said, "I'm Amelia, pleased to meet you."

"How long have you been working here, Amelia?" Shaun asked. He looked at the kitchen area where the drivers were laughing and loitering. He was dying for some drugs and put a wrap of cocaine right on the glass table. Bella, the madam stopped him. Suddenly a vibration interrupted the conversation. It was Shaun's mobile phone. In an attempt to answer the phone, he mistakenly punched the speaker button on the phone in his pocket.

"Hello, are you alright?" There came a woman's voice. "Where are you?"

"I'm in the cab office," answered Shaun. "My cab will soon be here." He switched off the phone immediately.

"Are you okay?" asked Giselle.

"I will be in trouble with my Mrs," replied Shaun.

Bella went to Shaun to explain the operations of the brothel. She said, "Pick a woman or women of your choice, an hour is £300 and you can pay by credit card with an additional fee of 30%.

"Which of them is your best pick?" Shaun whispered into Bella's ears.

Bella replied, "I am not allowed to recommend a woman for you."

Shaun pointed and said "Giselle."

Suddenly, three prostitutes came obtrusively into the lounge from upstairs and sat on the sofas. They had just finished an hour's session with a punter. The prostitutes were dazzlingly pretty, not simply exotic but shimmeringly beautiful. Their facial features were enhanced with high cheekbones, gorgeous blue eyes and a white skinned complexion. Their body proportions could be seen through the dresses. It showed they were as trimmed and fit as gym orderlies. They were in their twenties. It seemed unthinkable that they were prostitutes. They sat regally, their hands coyly laid on their laps, staring at Shaun.

Shaun smiled at them and said, "Hello." He found it impossible to turn down Giselle after he had struck a deal.

Giselle stared at Shaun and signalled for him to follow her to the bedroom. She held his hand, walked him up the stairs and led him into the bedroom.

Shaun was the chief executive of a global financial institution that stretched from China, across Europe, and to the USA and Canada; he was a rich punter.

Shaun said, "Don't we need to talk about money first?"

Giselle glanced at him and shouted for Bella to come upstairs.

"£300 an hour," Giselle said. "Bella will collect payment from you"

Shaun replied "Okay!"

Giselle asked, "Which country do you come from?"

"Originally, I'm from Australia," Shaun replied. "What's a beautiful girl like you doing here?"

Giselle laughed because she was used to such questions: a question commonly used to know a new girl better and understand her personality.

"That's a long story," she answered. Bella walked into the bedroom with a credit card reader. "How many hours do you want to stay?"

Shaun brought a Visa credit card out from his coat and gave it to Bella.

Shaun asked Giselle, "How many hours would you like to spend with me?"

"Five hours." Giselle answered.

Shaun then asked Bella to put the amount for five hours through the machine. It came to a total of £1,950. The payment went through; Bella then left the room.

Shaun took off his clothes, then looked as though he'd suddenly thought of something and said, "I'm dying for Charlie. I'll need couple of grams of cocaine."

"Okay," Giselle acknowledged. "I may have to call someone to bring it for you."

Shaun said, "I've got some." Soon, Shaun was already rolling cocaine on a £20 note.

Shaun said, "Please join me and let's get high together, it will make the sex better."

Giselle replied "Let me take a line so that I can fuck you hard." She pulled off her dress and got completely naked. Both of them sat on the edge of the bed taking the line. They sat facing each other naked. She came so close that Shaun could feel her breasts and placed her hands on his erection. Shaun turned around, for a moment there was silence; he didn't know what to say. Shaun asked Giselle to get a bottle of beer.

Giselle shouted for Mr. Freddie to bring a bottle of beer to the bedroom. Mr. Freddie walked into the bedroom and saw Shaun exploring Giselle's body with his hands. She was on top of him.

Shaun looked at Giselle groaning. She winked at Mr. Freddie and started to fuck him. Mr. Freddie opened the bottle of beer and left it on the table. Giselle grabbed Shaun, placed her hands on his cock and started to suck it until he screamed out.

Giselle went to the top drawer of the chest of drawers and pulled out a multi-function rampant rabbit vibrator. It was about twelve inches long, fully charged with new batteries. She stuck the vibrator in her pussy, turned it on full blast and asked Shaun to move it around. Shaun took hold of it and started to move it around inside her.

"Wow!" she shouted. After a few moments she put a coloured condom on Shaun and asked him to enter her from behind. Shaun and Giselle gazed at each other, as he fucked her doggy style.

"Fuck me, fuck me hard! She screamed out. "Don't stop." When she came, she smiled at Shaun's face.

"I'm dying for a shower," Shaun said and went to the bathroom. "You can join me."

Giselle joined him in the shower. The bedroom shower was like a jacuzzi. "It's nice and steamy," she said, as he climbed into the shower stall. Giselle climbed behind him. He started to rub her tits.

"I like your big boobs," he said, overwhelmed by her nakedness.

"You've a lovely body!" Giselle replied, "Please wash my pussy the way you would like it, ready for you to fuck. I keep my pussy shaved clean because I feel sexiest when it is smooth. It makes it nicer for men to lick and suck."

Shaun held a wash-cloth between her legs, soaped up the pussy with soap, scrubbed it hard and rinsed the soap off. Then he lifted her left foot onto the side of the tub. He started to lick and suck the lining out of her pussy. He sucked her until she couldn't take it anymore. She started to climax and shouted "Shaun! Shaun!! Shaun!!!"

Can I screw you with my cock now?" Shaun asked.

"Yes" she replied, smiling at him. She quickly washed Shaun's cock and arse. She quickly lubricated her pussy with baby oil and then ran to the bed. She threw her pussy wide open waiting for Shaun to climb on top of her. The lubricated pussy would make it easier for Shaun to penetrate into her dried clitoris without injury. Shaun got into the bed, looked at her and climbed on top of her. His cock explored her clitoris and his mouth explored her breasts. The right breast was larger than the left one.

He put his cock inside her and started to fuck the pussy gently. Shaun said that the pussy felt as though he was in the centre of an ocean. Shaun continued to fuck her until she came to a climax. She screamed and exploded with orgasm. Her thighs were shaking with aftershocks as he lapped up all of her juices.

A few minutes later, Shaun sat on the edge of the bed, still naked, thinking of what to do next. He spoke to Giselle in a low voice. "I don't want go home."

Giselle replied, "Your time is over. If you want to stay longer, you have to pay for more hours."

He was exhausted anyway. Shaun grabbed his clothes and got dressed. Shaun said: "I need to go home. I will be in big trouble with my wife if I stay longer."

Giselle replied: "Yeah, is that true?"

Shaun said: "I need to go." He then walked down the stairs into the lounge.

Shaun said goodbye to everyone in the lounge and walked out of the brothel to the waiting cab of Bashir. His face was full of excitement as he entered the waiting cab.

Mr. Freddie went to chat with Bella. Bella was sitting cross-legged on the sofa watching a film with three of the prostitutes. As she raised her head to speak to Mr. Freddie, the doorbell sounded. Mr. Freddie swung round. Bella was already getting up to answer it. Bella opened the door, smiling. Bella recognised the man immediately. It was Mike, a regular punter. The prostitutes around paid no attention, and were chatting among themselves. Bella made a calming noise. "Oh, please introduce yourselves to Mike." The prostitutes then introduced themselves. Amelia stared blankly at him. She didn't know him as a regular punter, not to say whether he was a big fish.

"Could you please pick a girl?" Bella exclaimed vivaciously. Bella brought the credit card machine to collect payment. Bella asked Mike how long he was going to stay.

Mike replied with a smile full of excitement, "Three hours."

Bella collected his credit card, swiped it through the credit card reader and keyed in £1,080. The payment was verified and the counterfoil handed to him.

Mike said: "I like Amelia." Mike suppressed his excitement, as he'd suddenly seen the woman he had slept with on his last visit. At that time of the morning, the brothel was freaky. Mike raised his head, gave a theatrical glance in Amelia's direction and winked. He found Amelia's eyes glinting with what looked like a seductive mood. She cleared a space on the sofa beside her, leaned back in it and crossed her arms with the attitude of someone who was likely to be impressed by what she was about to hear.

Mike walked straight to Amelia. She glanced up and palmed the only space for him to sit down. He sat beside her on the sofa.

"Hello," said Mike. "What do you have to offer me?"

Amelia offered him a bottle of beer. She chatted to him and started to poke her breasts into his eyes. She spoke to him with fierce vivacity. "Do you want anything special? I'm here for you."

Mike looked at her. Amelia looked at him and said in her sexy, thin voice, "I'm horny."

"What do you mean?" Mike replied.

Amelia stood up, gazed into his eyes and literally dragged the well-organised Mike. She led him upstairs to the bedroom. Inside the bedroom, Amelia sat on the edge of the bed and Mike sat beside her. She slowly pulled off her dress. Amelia came so close that Mike could feel her breasts and her stomach against his back. She placed her left hand on his penis. For a moment Mike was silent for a few seconds. He imagined why Amelia was so open to him. He blamed it on her being on drugs or too drunk. Mike stared intently for a few minutes, overwhelmed by her beautiful body. He fell for it, full of uneasiness and embarrassment. After a few moments, Mike said, "I love your beautiful body!"

Amelia was naked while Mike viewed her body and the bedroom with a dazed expression. The window was slightly open for air to come in. It had brocade drape curtains, a double-sized bed with no headboard, a glass table, a standing fan and a table lamp. A bowl of brilliant flowers was on the glass table. A rug sprawled on the floor, and on the hanger hung a white towel, pink bathrobe and shawl. A picture of a naked woman hung on the wall.

The bedroom was beautiful; perhaps it was because Bella, the madam was very stylish. The bedroom smelt of freshly–sprayed fragrance.

She grabbed Mike and pulled out his cock. She started to suck and lick his cock and balls. A few minutes later, Mike was grunting, moaning and groaning. Certainly, he was enjoying it. Amelia quickly pulled an oversized vibrator out from the drawer. She asked Mike to put it inside her. Mike pushed it in inch by inch.

Amelia shouted "Oh! Oh! Oh!" several times, a feeble cry full of trembling ecstasy. With no pity Mike was clutching the oversized vibrator inside her.

Bella went up and glanced into the bedroom; she was ashamed of the thickness of the vibrator. On the face of Mike shone a mirthful expression. Bella stared at him, surprised at what she saw and, not comprehending it, she felt embarrassed. She laughed; the oversized vibrator had provided her with laughter. Amelia looked at Bella, laughed softly and innocently. She was well pleased with herself.

When Mike's time was up, he came down to the lounge with Amelia. Mike walked straight up to Mr. Freddie in the kitchen area and said: "If you don't mind asking, what's the name of this place?"

Mr. Freddie replied: "Freddie's."

Mike took out his hand to shake his. Mr. Freddie reciprocated.

"How was your night?"

Mike smiled: "I've had a great time with Amelia." He requested Amelia's phone number, instead Bella gave him the brothel's contact number and asked him to ring the brothel whenever he needed to speak to her. He nodded his head in agreement and signalled to his driver for them to leave. He kissed Bella and said goodbye to everyone. Bella opened the door for him and he walked out of the brothel with his driver.

★ ★ ★

Business at the bankers' brothel was booming. Mr. Freddie had become a friend of one of the regular punters. This punter was a lawyer and a banker and worked in the city. He liked Mr. Freddie so much that he sometimes took him to strip clubs and paid for his drinks and dances. He was a man who had everything materially, nothing seemed to be lacking in his life. He was known to the bankers' brothel as Robbie. He was a man in his mid-fifties. He was a gentle, soft-spoken, medium-built man. Strangely, his cock was too big for a white man. Robbie would come to the bankers' brothel to look for Maya whenever he needed to offload his tension, whenever he was lonely and whenever he needed to take drugs. The lifestyle he had developed in his university years at Oxford was still embedded in him. He liked Maya because she took drug with him, fucked like a rabbit and when she fucked, the whole bedroom would shake as if there was an earthquake.

★ ★ ★

Robbie was at a strip club in the city. By 2am on a Friday morning, he had consumed about five pints of lager and had had over ten butt-naked dances. Robbie came out of a club and went straight to a cashpoint around the corner to withdraw cash. He was approached by Joe, a black male driver whom he did not know.

Joe said to him: "Do you want to visit the pretty ladies?"

Robbie replied, "Where?"

Joe answered: "It's just around the corner."

Robbie knew immediately and agreed. After he had drawn out his money, he followed Joe to his car and entered. Joe then drove him to the bankers' brothel at the mews. Joe pressed the doorbell. Bella, the madam saw them on the CCTV and a few minutes later she opened the door and ushered them inside. Robbie walked in and Bella held the door open for Joe.

Robbie stood for few minutes, glancing at the prostitutes seated on the sofa. He pointed at Maya. A few moments later, Maya stood up and gave him a brief kiss. She gently grabbed his hand and pulled him towards the kitchen area so that payment could be made to Bella.

Bella was sitting at the dining table with a group of black male drivers, all of them staring at him. Robbie felt uncomfortable but paid for a couple of hours to stay with Maya. He had picked Maya for his drugs not for sexual gratification. Robbie was a man who would go mad if he was not allowed to have his drugs.

After payment, Bella asked Maya to take Robbie to the bedroom upstairs. Maya led him through the stairs to the bedroom. They both sat on the edge of the bed, Robbie turned to face her and Maya moved into his arms fully. She melted against him, her legs against his and her finger rubbing the neck of his cock. Maya pulled her dress off so she was butt-naked. She offered Robbie a clothes hanger and a white night robe. Robbie brought out a small wrap of cocaine. He emptied the gram of cocaine onto the glass table in a straight line. He rolled a £20 note and used it as a straw to snort up the powder. Both of them took it and soon the effects of the cocaine were kicking in on them. Robbie stuck two of his left-hand fingers inside her pussy. Maya kept silent for a moment and grabbed his hand. She moved his hand up and down her pussy. She kept moaning and groaning. A few minutes later, he lifted her legs, spread them wide and buried his entire face in her pussy. Robbie sucked the lining of her pussy and ate her for ten minutes until she came like a volcano. She groaned, moaned and screamed out. She made sure Robbie got all her juicy pussy.

"Fuck me," she whispered to Robbie. Robbie stuck his cock inside her, moving his waist up and down, while she was shouting. Everyone downstairs could hear her and the bedroom was shaking. Suddenly, both of them moaned uncontrollably and screamed. They both had an orgasm at the same time. She got dressed and had a quick make-up. Robbie got dressed up too. Maya then led him down the stairs. Both of them came down the stairs into the lounge where Mr. Freddie was chatting with the drivers in the kitchen area.

Robbie stared at Mr. Freddie for few seconds. "Can you arrange for a cab to take me home?"

Mr. Freddie said he should sit down while he called his driver. Joe wasn't answering his phone, he had gone home. Mr. Freddie arranged for a taxi to drop him.

Robbie left the brothel late with a handshake and promised to call Mr. Freddie on his mobile phone.

The next day, Mr. Freddie sent a text message. "I hope all is well. How was the party?"

Robbie replied, "Mr. Freddie, thanks for sorting my cab to the station, I had a good evening. I feel terrible but cannot remember the name or number for the girl who I spent the evening with. Might be back tonight; what's her name? Sorry, too many chemicals and too much alcohol whizzing around my system."

Mr. Freddie responded, "Maya, the girl that fucks like a rabbit."

Mr. Freddie added, "When are you coming back for another party?"

Robbie: "Not sure. Was a little unhappy about the amount that was charged to my card last time for my visit about £1,150 which wasn't nice."

Mr. Freddie: "You are aware that an hour is £390. Work it out together with accessories."

Robbie: "Yeah, far too rich! I can party elsewhere for less. Shame as I have lots of clients in town who would like your place."

Mr. Freddie: "I can arrange a good bargain if you pay by cash."

Robbie: "OK. Look, I'm out on business for a few days. I have your number still, if you can come back with a better cash price I might give you a call."

Mr Freddie: "£250 an hour."

Robbie: "Blimey, that's a big mark-up for using a card for the amount of £420. I should get an hour and a half free!"

★ ★ ★

The brothel welcomed many punters. Two of the strangest visitors were a couple. Ben and Lauren worked in the city as bankers. Both worked long hours and earned a lot of money between them but never had time for each other and their sex lives had dwindled. The couple had been out at an event and ended up in a strip club in Shoreditch. Shortly after they came out to get a cab home, Billy, a black male hanging outside the door of the club offered to drive them home. He suggested the brothel to them as an after-party place to meet pretty women and have one last night drink. Ben spoke to his partner Lauren about the idea. The elegant, expensive and polished Lauren fancied the idea. Billy then drove them to the brothel.

Bella welcomed the tall, bald-headed man with the long-legged, slim, blonde woman to the brothel. Ben was as drunk as Lauren. There was an eerie strangeness about them. Bella invited them to one of the bedrooms, presented six prostitutes and asked them to pick. Lauren couldn't resist and chose Erika. Bella discussed the price for a prostitute while Lauren popped out to the bathroom to have a wee. Lauren came to the bedroom and ordered Ben to pay for Erika for two hours. She seemed to be in control of the night and Ben was just doing what he was told.

Ben took his credit card out of his suit, gave it to Bella and put through the payment for two hours. Bella and Ben came out from the bedroom to the lounge. They both sat on the sofa.

"Who is that lady?" asked Bella.

"It is my wife; we have been out drinking," replied Ben. "It was the driver's fault."

Lauren told Erika in the bedroom that she hasn't slept with her partner, Ben for six months. It had been going on like that for five years. They had become like brothers and sisters. She wasn't sure what was wrong.

"He doesn't want sex with me any more," she said.

Suddenly, Lauren pounced on Erika, grabbed her and said, "Please fuck me." They got naked. Erika started to feel Lauren's tits with one hand and grabbed her arse with the other hand. Erika went to the top drawer of the chest of drawers and pulled out a multi-function super rabbit vibrator. It was twelve inches long. The vibrator was fully charged with new batteries. She stuck the vibrator in her pussy, turned it full blast and started to move it around inside the pussy until the batteries went dead. She screamed all through the exercise. The batteries went dead after a long use. Mr. Freddie was sent to buy new batteries in the early hours of the morning.

Lauren turned to Erika and said, "I want a man. I've really wanted to do this for a long time, but haven't got a clue how."

Erika replied that they had a guy who came for that business. An hour later, a handsome white male prostitute entered the bedroom. He was called Pedro. Lauren asked Erika to call his partner. Ben came and paid for four hours on his credit card for Pedro and Erika.

Now, there were four people in the bedroom: Erika, Lauren, Pedro and Ben. Mr. Freddie came into the bedroom with the new set of batteries for the vibrator. The door was shut as soon as Mr. Freddie left the bedroom. Lauren kissed Ben tenderly on the softness of his lips. She needed a man but Ben couldn't be talked into making love, he was frightened of penetrative sex, ejaculation and orgasm. Lauren pounced on Pedro in the presence of her partner. She took off his pants and said softly, breathing into Pedro's ear "I need a hard fuck."

Pedro hesitated and looked at her partner, but he couldn't refuse; he had been paid. Pedro stood back and smiled at Lauren. Pedro smoothed his palms over her breasts and suddenly pushed two fingers up her pussy like a stick. Pedro asked her to bend down on her knees; he slipped his large cock in from behind. She felt the hardness nudging inside her. He started hitting her in a doggy style and slapping her arse. She screamed as if she was coming already. Pedro turned slowly, face to face with Lauren.

You could see in Lauren's face that this type of experience was entirely new and enjoyable. The orgasms were tipping over each other; they were seizing her body up.

"I want to release!" Pedro whispered.

"Oh! Oh! Oh," she screamed out as she had an orgasm. Ben was moaning and waiting to fuck his partner's arse.

Pedro came out, Ben entered and started to fuck her doggy style. Ben's concentration on this exercise was entirely a performance impossible to rehearse. Ben fucked her into submission.

"I love you, I love you," she screamed as she exploded again.

"Don't stop," Ben said. "I love you!" with his hands on her breasts and a kiss on her lips.

Lauren gave her husband a proud look and turned her head slowly, so she was face-to-face with Ben. She said: "What a wonderful experience. I love you."

She got dressed with a mixture of excitement and suspense. Lauren led them down the stairs to the lounge where Billy and Mr. Freddie had been waiting for the couple.

Ben said to Billy: "You're a good driver." Ben shook Billy's hands.

"Thank you."

Ben softly said, "Good bye" to Mr. Freddie and Bella before they left the brothel.

Despite the fact that Ben's wife had just been fucked by a stranger in his presence, he laughed and hugged her.

"I love you," he mumbled tensely. "I don't think what we have done was quite right, my dear. I really don't. That's dreadful. I think it was pressures from work.

Lauren raised her voice. "Great!" she hissed bitterly. Her mouth twisted into a childish grimace which, contrarily, served to make her appear more human and less twisted. "I'm very sorry, Ben."

He glared at Lauren, not trusting himself to speak. He finally managed to speak. "I have forgotten what happened," Ben said. "Let's put it behind us and leave it to one of those unusual experiences in life."

Mr. Freddie was puzzled by what he had witnessed. He felt he had entered a world of unreality. He couldn't connect or disconnect from the experience. The experience wasn't that funny.

Mr. Freddie was having a laugh over the incident with Bella when two punters, Gordon and Andy walked into the brothel with a driver. Gordon was an investment banker in the city, and regularly used the brothel to entertain his clients. Andy had missed his flight at Heathrow Airport after a business meeting with Gordon and was unable to get another flight. Bella offered them two bottles of beer and asked them to pick a girl. Gordon picked Eva, while Andy picked Maria.

The brothel was very busy that night and there was a shortage of bedrooms. Eva suggested that they should wait for the en-suite bedroom. Gordon and Andy nodded in agreement. They sat until the bedroom was made available for them. Eva led

Gordon, Andy and Maria up the stairs to the bedroom. The bedroom had a separate room with bath and toilet. Andy said he would prefer to have a shower with Maria. Maria was clean, since she had a shower earlier on in the brothel. Andy liked women with a soapy body and wet pussy. He wanted to have sex in the bath. Maria agreed and went with him to the bathroom. They showered together, she soaped him, he soaped her and they had sex, doggy style in the bath. When they had sex, Maria took control of affairs. She stuck her tongue in his mouth, she told him where to touch her and how. He fucked her until she had an orgasm. Andy had an orgasm at the same time she had an orgasm. Andy liked Maria so much because of the way she gave him such pleasure. Maria also enjoyed Andy.

"Second round!" Andy suggested that she should fuck him on top. She climbed on top of him, one of her breasts was on his open mouth and he used both of his hands against her bum. He stuck one finger into her arse and at that moment, she gave a toneless sobbing cry.

As soon as they had finished they went back into the bedroom to find Gordon in a deep sleep. He was exhausted after one round. No wonder, Eva had fucked Gordon as if nothing else in the world mattered. Gordon and Andy spent the whole night in the brothel with a settled bill of £9,800. Andy left the brothel to go straight to the airport while Gordon left for his office.

★ ★ ★

The brothel hosted so many strange clients at the time when bankers were awarding themselves huge bonuses. Another strange punter was Nigel. Nigel was known for his excessive spending and outrageousness. He was a short man, well below five feet. His most unsettling characteristics were his propensity to never shut up and the constant public use of the words 'fuck', 'cock', 'pussy', and 'blow job'. Dirty talk was the only way Nigel got his kicks and ejaculation.

One Monday night, he came to the brothel for a party. He had just been paid his annual bonus.

Monday nights were unpredictable: sometimes the brothel was busy and at times it was quiet. He was sitting on a sofa and talking dirty with Daisy, his favourite prostitute when Mr. Freddie walked into the brothel. Jokingly Mr. Freddie said "Hi freaky!"

He turned around towards him with an annoyed face.

"Hi," he replied.

Mr. Freddie offered him a handshake.

Mr. Freddie asked: "What is your name?"

Nigel replied, "I'm Nigel" before he was distracted by Bella, the madam.

Bella said, "Hello," smiling politely. "What do you want to drink?"

Nigel replied, "A bottle of beer, please!"

Bella gave him a bottle of beer.

Bella asked, "Could you please pick a girl?"

Nigel replied, "Girl?"

Bella said, "Yes."

Nigel replied, "I like all the girls here," but pointed to Daisy.

Bella led him and Daisy to the bedroom upstairs. Bella held a credit card reader to collect payment.

Nigel said, "I am a happy man; I've just been paid my bonus." Bella laughed. "Do you want more girls for the party?"

"Good question," he said. "Please bring me few of your best women."

Bella invited five more prostitutes to the bedroom.

Nigel picked Erika and Sophie. He said, "I like blonde women."

Erika and Sophie got naked. "What sort of music do you like?" Daisy asked, smiling.

Nigel replied: "I like a lot of older music, like Elton John, Boy George, The Who and Johnny Cash!"

"We like them too," the prostitutes replied.

He took out his credit card, gave it to Bella and said, "Charge any amount to this card."

Bella initially charged £1,080 but Nigel spent £10,500 in total that night on the prostitutes. He was fucked in a way that would last him for some time. He left the brothel with his face full of excitement.

Mr. Freddie bumped into him again a month later outside a strip club in the city. He had a handshake, went into the strip club and asked Mr. Freddie to wait. Twenty minutes later he emerged, checking his Rolex watch. He strolled towards Mr. Freddie, led him to his car, got in it and closed the door quietly. Mr. Freddie put the key in the ignition, kick started the car and drove to the bankers' brothel at the mews.

Whilst he was driving, he called Bella from his mobile phone to say that he was coming over with Nigel. When Nigel arrived in the brothel, he walked straight up to Bella and said, "I'm in a fucking mood. Where is Sophie?" Bella said that Sophie was in the bathroom and that he should wait for her. He sat on the edge of the sofa, smiled at the prostitutes and began to chat with Maya.

Nigel said, "How are you?"

Maya replied, "I'm Okay!"

Nigel said, "How was your night?"

Maya replied, "Fine so far."

Nigel said, "I want to open somebody's arse tonight."

Nigel was known for his dirty talk.

Nigel starred into Maya's sexy eyes. She smiled back at him. She stopped smiling when Nigel picked her.

Bella led Nigel and Maya to the bedroom and collected a credit card payment of £1,560 from Nigel. Maya smiled at him, began to undo his buttons and slowly ran her fingers down his chest to the top of his trousers. Nigel then placed his hand on her thigh; his face turned red as she lifted the towel she had tied around her waist to show her smooth, naked body. Maya waited patiently for Nigel to make a move, but he continued to stare at her. She leaned forward, climbed across him and lowered herself gently onto him. Nigel remained still on her as his cock was strong. Maya felt the hard cock inside her and then she began to move slowly up and down. She took his hand, placed it on top of her breast and left it there. Maya began to move up and down faster. Suddenly, he screamed out with an orgasm. A few seconds later, he fell into a deep sleep, exhausted. He woke up motionless. He dressed, dawdling and said "Goodbye".

★ ★ ★

There are more fascinating stories to tell about the brothel and what happened behind closed doors.

One of Mr. Freddie's little vivid recollections was that of a punter called Paul. Paul came into the brothel with a driver called Hassan. As Paul entered the brothel, he noticed drivers, mostly immigrants from Africa and Asia, chatting in the kitchen area. He spoke to Hassan, saying that he didn't want to be mugged. He said that he was afraid of black people. Mr. Freddie explained to Paul that the bankers' brothel was a safe place to cool off. He asked the drivers to leave the premises. The drivers and Mr. Freddie left the brothel immediately. A few hours later Mr. Freddie came back to the brothel. He could hear a sudden burst of excitement in the upstairs bedroom. For a moment he strained his ears to make out what the excitement was about, but he could hear nothing coherent. There were voices, someone laughing hysterically and sounds of some crawling.

"What could it be?" wondered Mr. Freddie. He hurriedly climbed up the stairs to the bedroom. Mr. Freddie wondered if there had been an accident or whether someone had been strangled. Mr. Freddie entered the bedroom. Paul was on his knees, naked; a rope was tied around his neck and he was being dragged around the bedroom. He was full of smiles when he saw Mr. Freddie. His body was full of bruises.

Mr. Freddie opened his eyes wide and closed them again, shivering. He screamed with anger at the prostitutes. "How dare you?" he yelled. "Do you want to kill him?"

One of the prostitutes replied to Mr. Freddie, "He's more used to this flogging than fucking. He pays for this kind of sexual act."

Mr. Freddie asked the prostitutes to stop. Paul gave Mr. Freddie a cold look. The look was particularly cold because he had been enjoying the flogging. Mr. Freddie would never forget the look. It was a look of intense hatred. Paul was clearly irritated by Mr. Freddie's moans and groans at the prostitutes. He put on his clothes and said "I'm going." He left the brothel in anger.

Meanwhile another punter called Howard was waiting to use the room. Howard was a regular visitor to the brothel, although Mr. Freddie didn't know if that was his real name. Howard was a lawyer/banker who worked in the city. He worked with controlled fury, drove himself hard and was always dressed smart. He entertained his clients in the bankers' brothel and at strip clubs in the night. He always worked late at night. There were days when he didn't see his wife, leaving home before his wife had woken up and returning home when his wife was asleep. When he came back from work late, shattered, he would creep into their bedroom without his wife knowing. He liked adventurous sex with prostitutes and spent a lot on the use of prostitutes. He spent an average of £5,000 whenever he came to the bankers' brothel. Howard liked to enjoy an abundance of everything: sex, alcohol and drugs.

On one particular day, he had been to a strip club in Soho with a couple of work colleagues. He left the strip club at about 2am, drunk. He had consumed a few pints of lager and had a few private dances. He was approached by a driver outside the strip club when he was looking for a taxi to take him home.

The driver spoke to him about the beautiful girls at the bankers' brothel, he agreed to follow him and was driven to the bankers' brothel. As soon as he walked inside the brothel, one of the prostitutes sitting on the sofa caught his eye. Giselle rose and greeted Howard with a kiss on the cheek. Her eyes gave the impression of something exciting and intoxicating. After a few minutes, Howard sat on the corner of the sofa beside Giselle. He looked at her, she smiled at him and he smiled back. Bella, the madam handed him a bottle of beer.

Howard said, "Thank you."

Bella asked him to pick a girl. Howard pointed at Giselle. Bella led Howard and Giselle into one of the bedrooms upstairs. Bella collected £600 cash from him for two hours. As soon as Bella left the bedroom, Giselle pulled off her dress, bra and pants. She beamed her tits at Howard's eyes. Howard got naked and sat on the edge of the bed facing Giselle and looking at her tits. "I want to eat you!" He spoke to her in a low voice. "You smell great!"

"Thank you," she replied, smiling at him.

"Can I have your pants?"

Giselle replied, "For what?"

Howard said, "I will pay for them."

Giselle repeated, "For what?"

Howard said, "I'd like to sniff your pants."

Giselle replied, "Well, I will take a generous offer."

Howard then gave her £200 for the pants. A few minutes later, Howard brought out a small wrap of cocaine. He snorted some cocaine to pep himself up. He rolled a twenty pound note and used it as a straw to snort up the powder. As the effect of the cocaine was kicking on them, he explored her body with his hands and mouth. He asked Giselle to bend down on her knees and started to fuck her from behind. Next the fifty-five year-old started to groan. He groaned throughout, while he was hitting Giselle hard at the spot with a lot of depth.

"Oh, Oh, please" she shouted.

Howard refused to remove his cock, as he was eager to show the power of a 55 year-old man's strength. He continued to fuck, fuck until he screamed and came with a bang. He kept his cock inside Giselle for a few minutes before he took out his penis. He sat on the bed imagining: what if she let me drink her pee? What if I let her tie me to the bed? He was contemplating extending his time with Giselle.

Bella came to knock on the door. "Your time is up," Bella said. "Do you want to extend your time?"

Howard replied: "You're too expensive." He dressed, kissed Giselle on the cheek and said, "Goodbye." He left the brothel with his face full of excitement.

Chapter 7
Prostitutes at the Brothel

There are thousands of prostitutes in London, where prostitution remains illegal. Just look in the local phone book or Google 'sex' on the internet, there are pages for prostitutes who'll come to your hotel room. Also, there are some hotels and strip clubs in the city that have their own girls.

Brothels proved invaluable to the sex industry, allowing prostitutes to make money in a secret location. The process for prostitution was easy, since opening legs did not lead to tragedy, but could make a prostitute become wealthy. The idea of brothels was to get rid of street prostitution and sex work in a brothel was considered safer than street prostitution. Previously, prostitutes would hang around on a busy street at night, waiting for a couple of hours to find a potential customer.

The sex industry is one of the many industries that operate in the shadow economy. It employs thousands of people and hundreds of business operators which provide sexual products and services. Business operators involved are brothels, escort agencies, sex shops and strip clubs. Brothels sprang up to meet the demands of the burgeoning sex industry. This has led many women to go into selling sex and the number of prostitutes has kept increasing. Some women sell sex for themselves so as to avoid handing over 50% of their fee to brothel owners and drivers. As a result, the prices for sex have fallen; instead of paying £300 for an hour at a brothel the punters can now go out and get the same service for a third of the money.

The sex industry had become decentralised that no one knew exactly its worth. Government sources value prostitution at £3 billion a year in the United Kingdom.

The law on prostitution in most countries has been uncomfortable and confused on how to manage it. Some prostitutes enjoy their job, and some do it unwillingly. Prostitution and the operations of brothels are legal in some countries, but illegal in others. There is no uniform policy and no consensus on the issue of prostitution. Laws on prostitution vary widely from country to country, influenced by the combination of many factors: medical, social, economic and religious.

In the Netherlands, the Dutch government had cleverly legalised prostitution. It has one of the most liberal prostitution policies in the world, and attracts sex tourists from many other countries. The profits from prostitution grew to enormous proportions contributing 10 million Euros to the European Union budget in 2011.

In United Kingdom, Italy and France, prostitution and the operation of brothels are illegal. It is very difficult for a person to operate a brothel without breaking the law.

In Sweden, Norway and Iceland, it is illegal to pay for sex. The client commits a crime, but not the prostitute. The famous Swedish laws of criminalising the purchase of sex mean Sweden provides some of the best protection to prostitutes who do it unwillingly.

In China, prostitution and the operation of brothels are illegal, treating the prostitutes as criminals.

In Thailand, prostitution is illegal but in practice it is tolerated; a sex tourist's destination for many countries.

In Pakistan, prostitution is taboo and brothels are deemed illegal but prostitutes operate underground.

In Australia, the operations of brothels is legal and regulated. According to a report in the *Australian Daily Telegraph,* illegal brothels in Sydney outnumbered licensed operations by four to one in 2009, while in Queensland only 10% of prostitution happens in licensed brothels, with the rest being either unregulated or illegal.

The Germans have very liberal prostitution laws. They have the largest brothel in Europe: Pascha in Cologne.

In the United States of America, prostitution and the operation of brothels are illegal except in rural Nevada.

In Japan, the operation of brothels is legal But placing the penis in the vagina is illegal·

In Brazil, prostitution is legal as there are no laws forbidding adult prostitution. It is illegal to operate a brothel.

In Nigeria, the operation of brothels is legal but not regulated.

In Egypt, Morocco, Libya and Tunisia, prostitution is illegal, but the laws that ban prostitution are ignored.

In Botswana, Namibia, Swaziland and South Africa, prostitution is illegal but it is a common practice partially driven by widespread poverty.

★ ★ ★

Mr. Freddie's idea for the brothel was to adhere to the principle "to protect donors of sex from abuse".

One of the prostitutes that worked at the brothel in the mews was Eva. Eva had a cluster of rich punters that allowed her to earn more than £50,000 a year. Eva was born in Latvia, but changed her name to Tracy when she came to London. She was a married woman with an elderly mother. Unfortunately her marriage had broken down leaving her single with no support.

Eva came to London after her university education and marriage broke down. She had a full-time job at a motorway service station. She worked shifts so she could send money back home to her old mother. But she had recently been made redundant, and she had been doing everything she could to find another job. During that time, she was really struggling with life in the United Kingdom. She was unable to afford the cost of living. She needed money quickly.

She met a friend, Erika. Erika was a woman she had known for a long time. Erika worked as a prostitute at the bankers' brothel. Erika arranged for her to work as a prostitute in the brothel. Jobs as an off-street prostitute were numerous and readily available. The prerequisite was to have a beautiful body and attractive boobs.

She had never smoked or been a drinker of alcohol. The old mother meant everything to her. That meant that to make money as a prostitute, she had to take lessons in how to drink, how to dress, how to show her tits and how to approach clients.

She got the tips from Erika. Eva's first night as a prostitute happened to be good night. She made enough money to spend and to send home.

Erika was known for her struggle to survive in life. Erika was a bright and pretty woman with a marvellous sense of humour. In Brazil, she'd been a fashion designer.

She had come to the United Kingdom with the dream of making money to support her family. Her whole life had been a struggle. She had to fight, month after month, against obstacles that would depress any unemployed young woman.

She fought it and the struggle had made Erika wealthy at the bankers' brothel. Erika wasn't her real name, Mr. Freddie came to know later. She gave herself that name when she started to work as a prostitute in the shadow economy.

Mr. Freddie discovered some of the excitement she'd found in prostitution. She had been a depleted and distracted little baby girl. At the first time, she found herself questioning the spoor of decisions that had led her to prostitution. Erika revealed her true story of what went wrong when she was a baby. She was a desperately lonely baby from a poor family. Her parents couldn't afford school fees; instead she got married early at the age of seventeen. She had no choice, when she was hungry, she hadn't any idea where the money to buy food would come from. It was the husband that sent her to study fashion design at a college.

As a married woman, every time she thought about starting a family life, she had always come up against the hard realities of a series of miscarriages. Eventually, she was pregnant and had a baby girl. She came to the United Kingdom on a tourist visa. She was to spend four weeks in London. Deep down in her mind she wanted a better life for her only daughter. She had already heard from friends that the UK would offer her a better life. Soon after her arrival, she became a prostitute. Erika would hang around outside hotels and strip clubs in the city. When she saw a potential person, she would signal the person for sex.

She became familiar with the cabbies who worked at these clubs and hotels. She was well-liked, her jokes made everyone laugh. Sometimes, when she was not busy, she would be driven to other strip clubs to look for clients.

Erika liked to say, "I want to make as many men feel good as I can."

She loved her job as a prostitute for three reasons. Firstly, sex is a natural human need, the same as the need for food and when the urge for sex strikes, is just the same as people going to a restaurant when they're hungry. No matter how much people are told that they will go to hell for having sex outside a relationship, men will have natural sexual desires and pay for it. Erika was not affronted to sell it.

Secondly, Erika used prostitution to solve men's health and psychological problems. The penis was a body part that she enjoyed to service.

Thirdly, Erika enjoyed sex for the money.

Mr. Freddie remembered one of her regular clients called Brad. Brad was a man of two centuries: modern and old. He was an elegantly cultured and highly principled man with a good sense of humour. He liked weird sex. Mr. Freddie wondered why Erika was having frequent sex with him. Erika once said that she had never seen a cock as big as Brad's. The cock looked more like someone's extra arm than a cock. He had once lost a condom inside her. She was comparing his cock to the many she had seen.

Erika was so nice that no cabbies criticised her courage and character. With the help of one of the cabbies, she set up her own brothel. She ran the brothel for a few months until it was shut down.

Despite the hurdles in the shadow economy, Eva and Erika turned their upside-down lives right again.

Chapter 8
The Last Day of the Bankers' Brothel

We all play our part in the drama of life. Mr. Freddie was no exception. Monday, October 18, 2011 was a day that started like any other day for Mr. Freddie. But it was the day the bankers' brothel at the mews was closed down.

The night Mr. Freddie was arrested was remarkable. Usually, he would not go to the city on a Monday night. He would do things about the house, play with the kids, watch Monday's live football match.

He was lured to the city by a punter called Jesuit. The punter had been to the brothel the previous week, had sex and caused a problem. It was a busy Thursday night. He had paid for 30 minutes to have sex with Maria. He couldn't ejaculate before his time was up. Maria left the bedroom to attend to another punter. Jesuit was extraordinarily furious. He complained to the madam and boasted that he was going to close down the brothel. Mr. Freddie intervened and decided to make it up. He picked another prostitute for one hour. He had no more money on him, so he requested for credit from Mr. Freddie. Mr. Freddie paid the madam for an hour on his behalf for Maria. Jesuit then promised to come to the brothel the following week to settle his account with Mr. Freddie. Maria led him to the bedroom upstairs. After a series of blow jobs he ejaculated, fucked and came with a bang. He was happy, gave his business card and asked for Mr. Freddie's number. Bella gave him Mr. Freddie's T-Mobile number.

Bella wrote the number on a piece of paper, in return he gave his credit card to hold to demonstrate his honesty.

On Friday, Mr. Freddie sent a text to Jesuit to remind him of the transaction.

Mr. Freddie sent, "Hi J, I hope all is well. Could you please arrange to transfer the £780 to my account?"

Jesuit replied: "Mr. Freddie, if it is OK, I would like to settle the bill on a credit card. Do you have the facility to take the details over the phone?"

Mr. Freddie sent, "No."

Jesuit replied, "Apologies, I am in Nottingham for the weekend."

On Monday, Mr. Freddie sent a text message to Jesuit to find out whether he was back from Nottingham.

Mr. Freddie sent, "Hi Jesuit, I hope all is well. Can you come down tonight to settle your account?"

Jesuit replied, "OK. Would you send me your address?"

Mr. Freddie sent, "I will be able to pick you up from anywhere in the city when you're ready to come tonight."

Jesuit replied, "Would you be able to pick me up at 10:00pm in the city?"

Mr. Freddie sent, "Yes."

Jesuit replied, "Are you able to pick me up at 10.45pm outside the Chancery Court Hotel on Holborn?"

Mr. Freddie sent, "Yes, see you later."

Jesuit replied, "Send me a text when you are outside the hotel."

Mr. Freddie left his home address at 9pm without telling his wife. He loaded up the boot of his car with cartons of beer. He sent a text message to Bella, the madam, to be at the brothel at 10pm. He also sent a text message to one of the card boys to be at the brothel at 10pm. As Mr. Freddie was driving to the city, the wife called on his mobile. She asked, "Where are you?"

He replied, "I'm going to the city."

"Be careful," she warned. "I don't want you to get into trouble. Please watch what you're doing and where you go."

Mr. Freddie replied, "I will not be in any trouble. I will see you later before 1am."

Mr. Freddie drove straight to the hotel. He arrived at 10.30pm. Inside his car, Mr. Freddie sent a text message to Jesuit.

Mr. Freddie sent, "I'm here."

Jesuit replied, "There in two minutes."

Jesuit got into the car. Mr. Freddie pulled away from the kerb unperturbed and drove to the brothel. A five minute drive to the bordello at the mews. Mr. Freddie and Jesuit went inside the brothel. Jesuit walked straight to the madam in the kitchen area and paid cash to settle his account. He immediately spotted Tracy. She was holding an over-sized vibrator. Jesuit pointed, laughed and walked towards her. Tracy was a real beauty, blonde hair, blue eyes, beautiful nose and silicon tits and she was wearing a high-fitting black dress. Tracy held Jesuit's hand and led him to the bedroom. She vigorously gave him a blow job. Jesuit was grunting and groaning until he came. Jesuit came out from the bedroom smiling pleasantly.

"Tell me you had a great time!" said Mr. Freddie, nodding his head at him.

"Yes, I did," Jesuit answered. Mr. Freddie led him out of the brothel to take a cab home.

So after Jesuit left the brothel, Goldie a cabbie came with a regular punter. His name was Jack. Jack said that he had been heading to a strip club when he was stopped by Goldie. Goldie, an African immigrant, aged 41, had short shaven hair, was carrying a golfing umbrella and wearing a camel-coloured coat and a scarf. He told Jack that the strip club shut at 2am and immediately asked him if he wanted to get "some pussy". Goldie went on to say that freddie's place was still open if he was interested. He declined the offer and went into the strip club. He remained in the club for an hour. It was raining heavily that night. Goldie, with his golfing umbrella, immediately approached him when he was leaving the club. He again offered to take him to Freddie's club. Jack accepted the offer. He walked with him for a short distance until he left him to get into his car. Inside the car, Goldie told him that the place he was taking him to was better than the strip club and that he could get "sex and a blowjob".

He made a telephone call to Bella, the madam at the bankers' brothel. He said "Hello, how many girls do you have on tonight?"

The madam replied, "Ten."

Goldie replied, "Do you have room for one gentleman?"

The madam replied, "Yes."

Goldie said, "Good. I will be with you in five minutes." Goldie drove him to the brothel at the mews and parked. Goldie knocked on the door. Mr.

Freddie opened the door and beckoned Goldie and Jack inside. Jack and Goldie walked inside the brothel. Mr. Freddie and Goldie then went to the kitchen area of the open-plan ground floor of the brothel, where several other drivers and girls were hanging out. At the general sitting area, three girls were sitting on a sofa.

Bella went to Jack and asked if he wanted a beer. Jack said, "Yes." Bella gave him a beer from the fridge in the kitchen area. The prostitutes introduced themselves to him one by one and sat down. Bella asked him to pick one of the girls. Mr. Freddie was still in conversation with the drivers in the kitchen area. Jack picked Erika. Bella took a credit reader and led Jack and Erika up the central spiral staircase to the first floor bedroom.

Bella said to Jack inside the bedroom, "Are you paying by cash or card, love?"

Jack replied, "Card please."

Bella asked him for his credit card and said, "One hour by card?"

Jack answered, "Okay" and gave her his credit card. Bella charged £390 to the credit card. After Jack entered his PIN number on the card reader, the card was declined. Bella asked him if he wanted to go to a cashpoint.

Jack said: "No, I have cash."

Bella replied: "£300 for cash."

Bella left the bedroom and asked Erika to collect the cash.

Jack then gave Erika the £300 in £20 notes. Erika left the bedroom with the money and gave it to Bella. She returned to the bedroom a couple of minutes later, holding a blue carrier bag. She told Jack to take off his clothes. Jack stripped down to his boxer shorts, while she stripped down bare naked. She placed her hand on his penis through his boxer shorts and said, "Please take your boxers off?"

Jack said, "Please let me keep them on for now."

She started to massage Jack. She then emptied the contents of the blue carrier bag out onto the bed. She brought two sealed condoms and a bottle of lubricating oil ready for a blow job and sex. Jack lay on his front with a hard-on, Erika sat astride him and she started to massage his back. His face was full of excitement.

After 10 minutes, Erika said: "Do you want Charlie, to make the sex better?" She put her finger to her nose and sniffed at the same time.

Jack replied, "I don't think I've enough money. I've only £45 left on me."

Erika said, "Give it to me and I'll see what I can do."

Jack declined the offer and she continued the massage. She pulled his penis from the boxer shorts and said, "I want your penis inside my pussy."

Jack replied, "I just wanted to continue with the massage."

Erika said, "You have family, you don't want to do sex, that's okay," and pointed at Jack's wedding ring.

A few minutes later Bella came to knock at the door to tell Jack and Erika that their time was up. Jack and Erika got dressed and led him down the stairs to the kitchen area where Mr. Freddie and Goldie were chatting. Goldie collected £150 from Bella for his commission and then took Jack outside the brothel. After that, Mr. Freddie left the brothel and drove to his office nearby.

On the walk to Goldie's car, Jack told him that his credit card had been declined.

Goldie said, "I think they had a problem with it, other people couldn't pay either." Goldie offered to take him to another brothel "around the corner" but he declined. Jack got into the car with Goldie and was dropped off at the Chancery Lane Tube Station. He charged him £28 for the cab fare.

Two hours later, Jack and his friend knocked on the door. Bella opened the door for them. She said angrily, "You should have called me before you came." Bella opened the door fully and said, "Hurry up, come in."

Jack stepped into the brothel and his friend held the door open behind him. Police officers who were in their cars quickly walked up to the door and entered the brothel shouting, "Police! Stay where you are!" and started to secure the occupants on the brothel. Inside the brothel were ten working girls (prostitutes), two drivers, the madam and the police officers. One of the drivers was Mohammed. Mohammed told the policemen that he was a taxi driver and he had just brought a man from the local strip club to see the girls and was waiting for him to finish.

As soon as the brothel was secured, what happened next happened quickly. Mr. Freddie was grabbed at his office in Hatton Gardens and taken to Holborn Police Station for interrogation. He was interrogated for 72 hours. Mr. Freddie had nothing to say during the interrogation. He knew straight away that people gossip and his fate had picked him out to crush, hurl and spit upon. Many owners of brothels in the city of London went unpunished. After all, the majority of the brothels in the city were overlooked, the bankers' brothel has been in operation for five years and a good number of his clients were the police.

He was charged with two counts; one of the charges concerned conspiracy to control prostitution and the second charge involved conspiracy to transfer criminal property. Mr. Freddie pleaded not guilty on the basis that the girls were willingly working for themselves as prostitutes and the women that worked in the brothel were not abused or trafficked. He said that the joint was solely for massage and he wasn't aware that sex was offered inside the bedroom. He was remanded in custody for three weeks. He became a vulnerable criminal waiting to be poached by legal aid defence lawyers.

The date for the court hearing was set. The trial was in Southwark Crown Court in Central London. At the trial, Mr. Freddie was accused of conspiracy to control prostitution and transfer criminal property on the basis that information was received that off-street prostitution was occurring at a premises in Holborn for which customers would be taken by taxi drivers, and that the taxi drivers would effectively tout customers from local strip clubs in the area and take them to the premises on the promise of sex. The customers would be charged £300 per hour, the taxi drivers would receive £100, the prostitute would receive £100 and the brothel would receive £100. Payment via credit card reader was also offered at an increased rate of 30%.

The evidence presented against him was overwhelming: text messages, witness statements, bank statements and e-mails.

There were two written statements from two undercover officers. One said that he went to the brothel on two occasions. On one occasion he paid £300 in cash for a girl and £60 for cocaine. On the second occasion he paid £390 by credit card and also paid for two grams of cocaine. The second undercover officer said that he went to the mews and the door was opened by Mr. Freddie. According to him, he tried to pay for sex by credit card but was declined and paid £300 in cash.

One of the prostitutes was interviewed. She said that Mr. Freddie was the boss of the bankers' brothel and clients paid £300 per hour for a girl. Girls had choice of what sexual services they provided for client. Payment sheets had 'Dr' for driver, 'G' for girl and 'H' for house.

One written statement was from a client of the bankers' brothel. The client was a city banker in one of the leading High Street banks. He went out for a work party in the City one Thursday evening. He ended up in a strip club near Holborn. He was kicked out of the strip club as he was drunk. He was approached outside the club by a black male driver. The black male driver said, "Do you want to go for another drink?" He agreed and went with him in his car to a mews property in a cul-de-sac. He got talking to a young woman who told him she was 22 and from Hungary. She was an attractive girl. He said he didn't know if someone spiked his drink, that the next thing he remembered was being in a small room alone. But he remembered being back to the lounge talking to cab drivers who told him that they were Ghanaians and Nigerians. He left with one the drivers. He was surprised that when he walked out of the brothel it was now daylight. He was on the train going home when he was called on his mobile phone by his bank to inform him that they had rejected two transactions believing that they were fraudulent transactions. They also told him that two transactions had gone through and been debited from his bank account. He cancelled these payments from his account and reported the matter to his local police station. The bank reversed the cancellation and paid all transactions as they believed that the transactions were not fraudulent. Just imagine, he had forgotten the girl he had fucked all night. The girl complained that he was a hard fucker and her pussy was sore.

There was a series of text messages as evidence. One of the text messages was a conversation with a punter known to the brothel as Ginger.

Mr. Freddie: "Hi, I hope all is well. There was a problem with one of the bank transfers. It is for £1,600. Could you please re-transfer? It was nice having you. Please I need a tip for being an errand boy. You're welcome to the mews anytime."

Ginger: "Hey Mr. Freddie. Sorry, I've checked my bank and credit cards and everything went through. I don't know how but I spent over £6.5k. I don't know what else you want from me, sorry. And I'm in big trouble with the credit card company!"

Mr. Freddie: "You used your NatWest debit card for the three transfers. I think the one for £1,600 was not confirmed. Those girls need their money. Please help me out. I promised to arrange a free session for you."

Ginger: "I'm sorry Mr. Freddie, but I have checked and it all went through there must be some kind of mistake. I really don't want to cause any problems but as I said everything I did went through and I spent over £6.5k on the night."

Mr. Freddie: "It did not go through. The ones for £1,500 and £1,640 went through. The transfer of £1,600 did not. Total for 12 hours spent."

Ginger: "Can you text me your bank details again and I'll try to take care of it!"

Mr. Freddie: "No need. Payee has already been set up."

Ginger: "Right, have just transferred £1,600. It's says it will be there today. Can you let me know when you get it so I know we are all cool? Thanks."

Mr. Freddie: "Thanks, the transfer went through. Please come to the mews anytime for free one-hour sex therapy."

Ginger: "Good, I'm glad it's all sorted out. Can you do me a favour and make sure my phone number is not on any mailing lists please, I'll be in trouble if I keep getting texts all the time! I have your phone number if I need to get hold of you. Thanks."

Another text message was a conversation with a prostitute looking for a job.

Girl: "Hi, Mr. Freddie, how are you? It's me, Paola, Brazilian. I already did some work for you, some months ago. I'm back in London now. I'm looking for a place. Can I work in your place, please? I feel secure in your place. Thanks."

Mr. Freddie: "Which Paola?"

Paola: "I'm Brazilian, long blonde-coloured hair, blue eyes, and size 10/12. I worked in your place before I travelled to Brazil."

Mr. Freddie: "Can I see you tonight?"

Paola: "Hey Mr. Freddie, thanks for your reply, but want u to "see" me or I'm coming to work tonight?"

Mr. Freddie: "You can work tonight, usually not busy on Monday."